After Church Mysteries

Rev. Richard Burgess, P.I.

a novel in stories

by

WILL MARTIN

ISBN-13: 978-1535548083
ISBN-10: 1535548088

For Jeanne

First. Forever.

Table of Contents

And Where Will You Be Staying?

(Part One)

Had I been as alert as I soon would be, I would've put on my pants. But I wasn't, and I didn't. Next thing I knew, I was waking up from a prone position on the floor, blood dripping on my tighty-whities and with a hankering for Fritos.

My first day of my first week of retirement had begun beautifully, highlighted by an available window seat on Southwest flight 111 from Hartford to Tucson. I tugged the *New Haven Register* out of my carry-on, stuffed the L.L. Bean bag into the overhead compartment, and climbed into my favored window seat. I found the article I'd been reading – an interview with me – when boarding began. Ego aside, I dreaded stories about me – misquotes seemed obligatory. This one was no different. "Rev. Burgess said the decision to retire after thirty years from the Hillsdale

Community Church was the result of his getting tired of the parishioners."

"Not! *Not* the result of.…" I could hear the usual suspects burning up the phone lines now. I wouldn't miss that, I'll tell you.

Clear your head, Richard, I lectured myself. Truth is, the reporter got it right, and you know it. You *were* tired of the people. At least a lot of them. Enough to put the church in the rearview mirror for good.

I was about to switch my iPhone to airplane mode when it vibrated. Mary Ellen.

"Dickie, I've been receiving calls about the *Register* article. Did you see it?"

Only my wife of 30 years could get away with calling me Dickie. "Yes, I saw it. Pretty good picture, don't you think?"

"Well, is that what you said? About the church people?"

"Of course not. At least, I don't think so."

This was good: the stewards were coming through and slamming shut all the overhead bins. From experience, I knew this was the same as firing a starting pistol for the pilot to get things moving.

"But what should I say?" Mary Ellen continued. "Winnie called all atwitter about it. Said you'd been living a lie. Said she'd never have put the church in her will if she'd known you felt this way."

"Say it was a misprint. They'll find something else to be atwitter about tomorrow. And remind her I'm no longer the pastor. Take it up with the new one they hired. Oh, geez."

"What's the matter?"

"Nothing, I've got company," I whispered. "I'll check in when I land."

"Bet you thought you were going to have the row to yourself, huh? Sorry."

At least my seatmate was a thin woman. Hard to tell her age. Thirty-fiveish. Latina, lovely dark hair falling where it wanted, making where it wanted to fall seem perfect.

"Where you going?"

"Tucson," I said.

"I know you're going to Tucson. The whole plane is going to Tucson. I mean where are you going in Tucson?"

In a few seconds I'd gone from having the row to myself to entertaining a Chatty Cathy on caffeine.

"I'm going to a conference," I lied. I'd learned long ago that revealing my clergy status too often led to bad things happening to good people – me. Either I got an earful of their problems or a gasp that suggested they considered me a sexual predator. But I hadn't thought about what to say when that time came.

"So, what do you do?"

That time had come. "Uh, a detective. I'm going to be a detective."

"Going to be?"

"I'm going to be a private investigator – after some training."

"A private dick, huh?"

I don't remember if I said it aloud – *"Here we go."*

"What's your name?"

"Richard. Richard Burgess."

"Oh, so a private dick named Dick. That's cool."

I didn't think anybody but mystery writers referred to PIs as "private dicks" so this threw me. "I don't go by Dick," I said. "I prefer Richard, if you don't mind."

"Works for me," she said. "Richard, Dick, whatever."

The plane had begun inching away from the terminal. Soon we'd be in the air and five hours later in Tucson. I wanted to end this conversation.

But I couldn't. Old clergy habits of niceness die hard. "So why are you headed to Tucson?"

"I'm going home. Have been visiting friends in Bristol. I like Connecticut. You live here all your life?"

"Yup."

"So what did you do before signing up to be a dick, Dick? Er…Richard?"

"Worked in communications, sales end of it." That wasn't so bad. Why hadn't I thought of that years ago? "You live in Tucson?"

"No, but not far from there. Ten miles from Lester Moore," she said with a laugh.

I knew Arizona had many Spanish named towns, but I'd never heard of Lester Moore, which didn't even sound Spanish. Honestly? I didn't care. I really didn't care. I can't tell you how much I didn't care.

Mercifully, she was distracted by the little boy behind us kicking her seat, and her need to give the kid a mean stare. I picked up the *Register* from my lap and finished the article in solitude. It was harmless enough except for the quotation that had aroused the "atwitter" people. And the picture was good, darned good. Though the angle wasn't perfect. Made me appear as if I had a pot belly. I glanced down. Well, can't stay in football shape forever.

As if she were following my gaze, she said, "What's that on your shirt?"

Good grief. "I don't know. Ketchup, I suppose," I said. "From the Quarter Pounder at the airport. Or the fries."

"You should wipe it off," she said. "You want some water?"

"Mary Ellen always says that makes stains worse."

"Here, I'll daub it off with a tissue. There. At least it's not so noticeable. You don't want to show up for private eye school with ketchup on your shirt."

"Thank you," I said, thinking about when I'd be able to change shirts. The weeklong course in "So You Want to Be a Private Investigator" began the next day, and I hadn't allowed for accidents. Either getting it cleaned or picking up a new one were my only choices – you'll find I'm quick with decision-making.

"Where's your gun?"

"My gun? I don't have a gun," I sputtered. "I hate violence."

"You a religious fanatic or something?"

"Not really. Just a minister." I've always had this compulsion to tell the truth, and it had gotten the better of me. If I was going to make it outside the church, I needed to learn better how to lie. I'd have much preferred to be known as a religious fanatic on this occasion. Or even a predator, for that matter. As it was, I could only hope she was the kind who'd be put off by my reverend status and leave me alone. I was wrong.

"So, Dick – Richard – why'd you lie to me before?"

"I've just had bad experiences on airplanes telling people I'm a minister. Of course, I'm not one now. I mean I'm still ordained, but I retired. Early retirement, you could say. I apologize for the misdirection."

"No problem. My uncle's a minister and he's in prison so I understand. Anyway, why's a nice minister like you going to private eye school?"

"I'm running away," I heard myself say. I'd apparently slipped into a "tell the truth" program and couldn't log out. "I'm just tired of a lot of stuff. I've had it with mothers of the bride who try to run weddings, with trustees who want to rent space to fortune tellers, with board chairs who think my car is too fancy, and with Fred who sits in the back row and complains every week – every single freakin' week – that he can't hear and that I should speak up." I wanted to confess more, but, frankly, I was shocked at myself. I couldn't believe what I'd told a complete stranger. I tried to pretty things up. "I love people. I do. Just burned out on the ornery ones. I've decided to try my hand at helping people in a different way. My dream is to set up my own detective practice in Connecticut. First, though, I've got to do this course and then be an apprentice to a PI for a couple of years. The Chief of Police back in Hillsdale is paving the way for me."

"My, my, you're the brave, adventurous one," my new confidante said.

"Not really. Just following my interests."

"How did your interests lead to detective work?"

I didn't have a good answer for her. Or for myself, for that matter. I grew up watching police shows on television, loved reading mysteries, maxed out on Robert Parker's private investigator Spenser novels. When Parker died, it was as if his sidekick from the 'hood, Hawk, hit me up side of the head; I wanted to continue Spenser's mission. Though I wasn't a tough guy like Spenser. And I didn't have Hawk. And I had no experience except for being a police chaplain. And I had this minister shtick going. Providentially, one might say, Mary Ellen inherited her folks' estate last year, which meant neither of us had to work anymore if we didn't want to. And we didn't want to. "It's a long story," I said. "You know, they say taking off and landing are the most dangerous parts of air flight. That's when 98 percent of all passenger deaths occur."

I swear I could see her knuckles getting white, contrasting attractively with her brown skin. I put my head back and hoped when we were airborne she'd have mercy on a sleeping parson.

***

"What would you like to drink?"

I'd dozed off. "I'll have a Diet Coke," I said to the flight attendant. "And what do you have to eat?"

I was well aware that Southwest only served snacks, but I always hoped one day I'd hear, "We've got this fabulous pepperoni pizza in the oven, and if you'd like I'll bring it to you."

Such are my fantasies. Mary Ellen says I think way too much about food. Still, I did have a yearning for whatever serving of pretzels or crackers or rock-hard cookies in a wrapper they had. I wanted my money's worth. I mean, I'm too much an old Yankee to settle for less than I'm paying for.

It was cookies today. My seatmate gave me hers. Wished it had been pretzels, but those are the breaks. After reclining her seat all the way, Lester Moore's neighbor was out of it until the pilot announced our descent into Tucson. I'd been watching a movie on my iPad.

"You've gone and done it again."

"What?" I asked, yanking my earplugs out.

"You've got cookie crumbs on your front," she said, sweeping them away with a hand.

"As my wife says, you can dress me up, but you'd better leave me at home," I said, an attempt at humor met by her gaze of incomprehension. "I never asked your name," I said, trying to regain some dignity. "I've told you more about my life in a couple of hours than I've told anyone in a long time."

"Jasmine."

"That's a beautiful name. What's your last name?"

"Jasmine is enough," she said.

I could take a hint. Wished I had willpower like that.

We had nothing more of substance to say to each other until we deplaned and headed towards the baggage claim area. "And where will you be staying?" she asked.

"Pardon me?" I answered, having tuned out anything other than my bag calling my name from the carousel.

"Where will you be staying in Tucson?"

"At the Grande Hotel here at the airport. The class is being held downtown so I'll rent a car. I can give you a lift if you live nearby."

"No, thanks. I've got a ride. It was nice to meet you, Richard. I hope we meet again, and that your school goes great and you always get your man or woman or whatever the case may be." And with a halfhearted smile, she left, her suitcase thumping along behind her.

CHAPTER TWO

My watch and my stomach said it was 6 PM, but the Arizona clocks said 3 PM. Daylight Savings Time in July for everyone but the state of Arizona. Go figure what that's all about.

I decided to pick up the car first and find a fast-food joint. Could have dined in the airport, I know, but I'd consumed enough airplane/airport food for one day. I'd had McDonald's earlier, so I passed that by. Taco Bell came next, and I pulled in. The music was blaring hip-hop, which I don't think is Mexican particularly. But I wasn't there for a concert. The Fiery Doritos Locos Taco Supreme caught my eye. I skipped dessert so I could tell Mary Ellen I did. And, miracle of miracles, nothing new fell on my shirt.

I'd left a message for my wife while waiting in line for the rental. As I pulled out of Taco Bell, my phone chimed.

"I've had several calls about the newspaper article," she said immediately. "And I explained that you were misquoted, but I don't think they believed me. Fred said he knew you hated the church a couple of years ago when you began whispering your sermons just so he couldn't hear them. And Winnie called back and said she'd phoned the new pastor, and he's much nicer than you are so she's not going to change her will. But she did say she wouldn't be sending us Christmas fruitcake in the future."

"Maybe you should screen phone calls for a day or two. We're not the first family anymore, and it's time they got used to it, though it doesn't sound like they're exactly having a pity party. I'm just pulling in to the Grande. I'll give you a ring tomorrow. Wish me luck."

I have sleep issues when I have to set an alarm. My doctor says it's some kind of anxiety. Maybe when I'm long out of the church business, it won't be a problem. But for now, if I want eight hours of sleep, I need to allow ten hours in bed. Still, I'm lucky to get four decent ones. Nevertheless, I set the alarm because the only sound sleep I manage is the last 30 minutes before it goes off. I attempted the math for tonight: *since class was to start at 8 tomorrow, which is 11 back home, and if it's now midnight at home and 9 here, and if a freight train leaves Chicago at 2, and a passenger train leaves St.*

*Louis...*I gave up, brushed my teeth, set the clock radio for 6:30, tossed the previous-occupants'-butt-tarnished bedspread on the floor, and crawled under the sheet.

It wasn't all that long after that I was awakened by a woman banging on the door and screaming my name. It was 1:17, which I immediately translated as being 4:17 back home.

Obviously not fully awake, wearing only underwear (my usual bedtime garb), I threw open the door, and who was standing there but Jasmine with no last name.

"Richard," she said as she fairly leaped into the room. "Shut the door and lock it."

"What the heck's going on? Please excuse me, where are my pants? Do you see my pants?"

"My boyfriend is crazy! He's abusive and extremely jealous and an absolute control freak. I told him about you, about the nice man I sat with on the plane, and he flew into a rage. You've got to protect me."

"Well, sure," I said, shifting into my highly trained pastoral mien. "But how'd you know where to find me?"

"You mentioned you were staying at the Airport Grande Hotel. I told the desk clerk I was your wife, and I'd forgotten my room number."

I wondered if my pants were under the covers on the floor. I'm not a particularly modest person, but I really didn't want to flash around in my tighty-whities any more than I had to.

I was on my hands and knees searching under the bed when again there was pounding on my door. Before I could ask, "Who is it?" Jasmine had opened it. I was about to meet Rusty.

"You slime ball," he said without extending his hand. "Jasmine says you're a minister. Hah! You're a disgrace. Keep away from my girl, you hear me?"

"Rusty, you don't understand," Jasmine began.

"I understand plenty. Look at him down on the floor in those little underpants, all bunched up. What have you two been up to so fast, anyway?"

I couldn't get up quickly enough. Or probably I could have, but I tripped in the covers and had to grab Jasmine for balance.

I guess that was what sent Rusty over the edge.

CHAPTER THREE

Lying there in my empty room on the aforementioned butt-tarnished covers, I had little memory beyond a big fist in my face so I supposed it must have continued its journey into my nose. My head hurt something awful, and, as I mentioned, I had the strongest craving for Fritos. And then the alarm went off. I needed to call the police, of course. I dialed 911, but apparently, I should have dialed nine first or something because I got Room Service.

"Buenos días," I said, trying to ingratiate myself with the nice Spanish-accented woman who answered.

"What?" she asked. "What did you say?"

"I said 'buenos días,' good morning," I answered. "I'm speaking Español."

"Speaking what?"

"Never mind. I was attempting to call the police, not room service. Can you tell me how to dial the police?"

"Why do you want the police? If the meal was bad, you can talk to the manager."

"No, the meal was...Actually I didn't eat anything, and I don't want to order anything...Hello? Hello?"

"For emergencies press 0," I now read on my phone guide. So I pressed 0.

"Front desk. How may I assist you, Mr., uh, Mr. Burgess? I do hope your wife found her way to your room last night, and your brother, too."

"Yeah, everything's just peachy. Look, I need to call the police. How do I do that?"

"Why do you need to call the police? Have you been robbed?"

"Wait a minute. I didn't think of that. Have to find my pants. Hang on."

One's pants are not hard to find when they've been tossed in the middle of the bed that you didn't get to sleep in. Wallet was there, but my MasterCard was gone, as was the American Association of Retired People (AARP) card from when I turned 50 a few years ago, plus library card, insurance cards, the kind of stuff you have in your wallet, I'm sure. Also missing was five hundred bucks in twenties. My driver's license was still in my buttoned shirt pocket from the flight check-in as was my AMEX card after swiping it at the airport McDonald's. Could have been worse. But, still.

"Yes, I was robbed. How do I contact the police?"

"I'm so sorry, Mr. Burgess. I'll call them for you. In the meantime, thank you again for staying at the Tucson Airport Grande Hotel. Is there anything else I can do for you? Did you know that members of our Super Savers Club save 10% on all purchases from the lobby newsstand with the exception of food items and newspapers? Sign up today. Stay on the line for the next available representative."

This was turning out to be almost as bad as a day at the church. I should call Mary Ellen.

***

"What woman? You were in your room alone with a woman in your underwear? Dickie, I can't believe this!"

"Calm down, calm down. I think I may have been set up. Or maybe Jasmine really was running from Rusty. I don't know."

"Jasmine, is it? Dickie, you haven't been gone 24 hours and you're taking up with a floozy? I'm so disappointed in you."

"Honey, it's not what it seems. I'll get back to you after I talk with the police. Okay? Okay? You still there? Hello?"

I must have missed the memo saying hanging up on people extends your life span or some such gem from Dr. Oz. It was happening a lot to me lately.

The police arrived shortly. I knew this because there was a polite knock at my door and, peering through the peephole, I saw a tall man and a very short woman in blue uniforms with badges pinned high on their pectorals. I opened the door and invited them in.

The woman glanced behind me, then fixed me with a stare. "I'm Officer Diaz, and this is my partner, Officer Blankenship. I understand you claim to have been robbed."

"Yes," I said. "Last night or more accurately early this morning. By two people. And I was punched in the nose and knocked out by the man, which explains all the blood you see on everything."

"How much do you claim they took?" Officer Blankenship asked.

"My billfold had five hundred dollars in twenty dollar bills. I got the money from my bank before leaving Connecticut. And my MasterCard. Plus, my AARP and other cards."

"Why were these two people, this man and woman, in your room in the early morning hours, Mr. Burgess?" Officer Diaz said while kicking aside the unhygienic covers as if a perpetrator might be hiding underneath.

"I'd met the woman on the flight out, and …"

"Mr. Burgess, please," Diaz said, now maybe an inch from my belly button. "I wasn't born yesterday and this isn't my first rodeo. And my partner may have been born at night, but not last night. Here's what happened, so let's just get on with it and stop wasting each other's time. You met this woman, invited her to your room for sex, and got beat up by her pimp because you wouldn't pay. Or you did pay, but then decided you'd paid too much, and thought by simply calling the police you might get your money back. Or salve your conscience. Or have a story to tell your wife. Or who knows what. Okay? So, can we stop with the 'I was robbed' crap?"

I tried to think of a cliché with which to respond. But I was coming up empty. "I know it probably looks like the situation is everything you've described, but I'm telling the truth. I'm a minister from Connecticut, and I've come out here for a class in private investigation. I would never solicit a prostitute."

"Oh, well, then, that's different," Officer Blankenship said. "I guess we're sort of comrades in the world of law enforcement, aren't we? Yeah, I was a doctor, myself, before deciding to enter this wonderful profession. And Diaz was the president of Mexico."

I may sometimes be slow to catch on to sarcasm, but I was pretty sure Blankenship was pulling my chain. "Okay, look, I have other things to do today," I said. "If you won't believe me, fine. Thanks for stopping by. And, by the way, I know for a fact that no woman has ever been president of Mexico." I felt badly for showing off my higher education, but they had it coming.

Diaz and Blankenship stayed just long enough to write down the "incident," as they called it. Advised me to contact MasterCard. They didn't seem to care about the AARP card.

I heard them laughing, or more aptly, whooping and cackling as they walked down the hall. One of them must have told a funny. Anyway, good riddance to bad rubbish. Darn, why didn't I think to say *that* when they were here?

My phone buzzed on the desk. Mary Ellen.

"Dickie Burgess, of all the predicaments you've gotten involved in over the years, this takes the cake. You'd better be telling the truth or so help me I'll never talk to you again. You need to pack your things and come back home. You are obviously incapable of living a normal life outside the church."

As she talked, I couldn't get the Fritos out of my head. I thought I'd seen them in the vending machine by the elevator. But now I had no money, and it probably wouldn't take American Express. I imagined there must be a bank nearby so I could pick up some cash. And the newsstand must sell Fritos even if I couldn't prove I qualified for a 10 percent discount.

"Are you listening to me, Dickie Burgess?"

"Yes, dear, I hear you. I'll be more careful in the future about whom I talk to. Say, listen: Can you cancel our MasterCard? And call the number on the back of your AARP card – I need another one. I have to go. I can still make the tail end of the orientation session. Please don't worry about me. I'll talk to you later. Love you."

After taking a couple Tylenol, cleaning up the room, and enjoying a long shower, I knew I couldn't do school. Not today. I had to find out if Jasmine was okay. If Rusty was abusing her, I had to do something. She'd asked me to protect her, and I'd agreed. I would have done the same for a church member. And Jasmine was much nicer than most of them.

CHAPTER FOUR

Ten miles from Lester Moore, she'd said. Where the heck was Lester Moore? Thank heavens for Google. My iPad query returned a top-of-the-page Wikipedia article for Boothill Graveyard in Tombstone, Arizona. Lester Moore was a man and apparently more famous for the inscription on his tombstone in Tombstone than for his life. He'd been a Wells Fargo station agent shot in the late 1880s because a customer was upset over a crushed package. Lester Moore's epitaph reads: "HERE LIES LESTER MOORE, FOUR SLUGS FROM A 44, NO LES NO MORE."

Humor even in death. I remembered Jasmine giggling when she said she lived near Lester Moore. A clue. That was a clue – I think I'm going to be a very good PI. Maybe she thought she was being cute, which meant Lester Moore as she used it was either a metaphor or a simile or a symbol. Or, are all similes metaphors, but not vice versa? But what about symbols? Or, of course, her titter may have derived from eyeballing the ketchup stain on my shirt once again. I was betting on the former, however.

Tombstone wasn't all that far from my hotel. An hour and fifteen minutes, according to Google. She hadn't said in what direction her home was, so I had to zoom out on the map that filled my iPad. There was only one town within ten miles of Tombstone, Sandy Creek. Of course, Jasmine didn't say she lived in a town. Might live way off any beaten path. But, I'd start with Sandy Creek, go nose around, and find a place to eat. Check out the lay of the land, as Spenser, my novel detective mentor, might say.

July anywhere in the United States can be hot. In the desert, "hot" didn't begin to describe what I experienced. My Camry kept me comfortable cruising down I-10 at 75 miles per hour, but it declared it was 108 degrees outside. Having been assaulted by the heat when I'd rolled down my window to obtain some cash from a drive-thru ATM, I didn't doubt it for a second. I'd seen a T-shirt for sale in the lobby newsstand declaring, "But It's a Dry Heat" and showing a skeleton in the desert. I could believe that, too. And, no, they didn't have Fritos.

The road changed dramatically as I left the interstate. Not a bad road, not at all, just a lonelier road. Hardly any traffic, fewer signs, and an abundance of objects that could have been skeletons in the desert amidst the cactus and other prickly plants. I'd been cautioned by the guy at the lobby newsstand to take plenty of water with me if I was going out. He said he'd give me 10 percent off if I were a Super Saver member. I told him I wasn't. He said he could put me on the phone with someone, and they could sign me up right then. I said no thanks, and he seemed crushed. As it was, a six-pack of Evian water set me back fifteen bucks. That didn't seem right, but I had to get going. I was on my first case, in a manner of speaking.

I'd picked up a color brochure next to the lobby newsstand for Tombstone that boasted it was "the town too tough to die." If I'd been sightseeing, I'd have been tempted to visit a couple of their museums, take in a gunfight at the O.K. Corral, and ask around to see if Wyatt Earp really was brave, courageous, and bold as the song says. But I was going to Sandy Creek on business.

Sandy Creek seemed aptly named, though there was no sign of a creek. But if it existed, it definitely would have been sandy. First, though, I needed to eat. The Sandy Creek Double R Bar Saloon and Chinese Restaurant caught my eye.

I was offered a stool at the bar in front of a large mirror, and while that would normally be a good place to sit – you can keep an eye on what's going on behind you, as Spenser would certainly do – today a booth by the window seemed more inviting. The pleasant, leathery-skinned server brought me a tall glass of ice-cold water and, as they say in the West, I was mighty obliged. When she came around again, I ordered an iced tea, no sugar, no lemon. I downed it immediately. I was trying to decide between the Gunfighter's Two-Fisted Sirloin Burger and General Tso's, and had about settled on the burger as long as it came with crispy fries when a young boy, maybe 10 or 11, came running into the restaurant. And right into my booth. And under my table.

I hoped Mary Ellen wouldn't call at that moment. "Son, what's the matter?" I said, pulling him up into the seat.

"A man tried to grab me. Said he wanted a Navajo boy," he answered. Then, accepting the invitation to join me, but huddling down so he couldn't be seen through the window, he added, "He was crazy. Had this wild look. Must have been drinkin.'"

"Where are your parents?" I asked.

"My mom's dead. My dad's at work. I'm supposed to stay home, but I wanted a cold pop."

"There you are, Tonto," said a wild-looking man, obviously drunk, coming out of the kitchen area, dragging two cooks, one on each arm, as he strode steadily toward us. "You come with me. Who's this guy?"

"My name is Richard," I said. "Richard Burgess. Are you related to this young man?"

"Am I related? Hell, yes, I'm related. I'm, uh, his uncle."

"No, you're not!" the boy protested. "You better get out of here before I call my dad. He'll beat you up."

"Look," I said, drawing on my experience with mentally unhinged, drunk parishioners, "let's be reasonable. I'm not going to let you take this boy if he says you're not his uncle. And that's that. So you might as well mosey on back to wherever you came from and sleep it off. Okay?"

It apparently wasn't okay, because for the second time in twelve hours, a punch was thrown my way. Unlike my earlier experience, however, I saw this one coming from its drunken, not-so-immaculate conception and easily blocked it with my left arm. Then, channeling my inner Spenser, I let fly a right to his chin that knocked him over a table in the center of the dining room. There he lay in a sodden stupor. Wow! That felt good! Except for the throbbing pain in my right hand. I hadn't slugged anybody since Tommy O'Boyle in the fifth grade. But I still had it!

"Call the sheriff!" someone yelled. Actually, that was my voice I heard.

"We ain't got a sheriff, you Yankee loser," a man wearing a bolo tie but no shirt said. "We got a marshal. There's only 500 people. Whaddya expect? A SWAT team?"

I would gladly have settled for a thank you.

"Thank you, mister," said my young friend, proving once again that the next generation is going to be better than the present. "My dad will want to thank you, too. Do you live here?"

"No, just passing through," I said, noticing that a southwestern drawl had found its way into my voice.

And I noticed something else. Not ten feet away on the other side of the glass was Rusty sauntering down the sidewalk.

CHAPTER FIVE

I didn't want to leave the young man, who said his name was Frankie, but I had to follow Rusty. The owner of the Sandy Creek Double R Bar Saloon and Chinese Restaurant assured me that he knew the family and would take good care of Frankie, who vouched for the man. He also said the iced tea was on him. If I could have gotten that in writing, I'd have had documentation from my first paid job to tack to a wall in my office whenever I got one. Still, the fact remained: I'd been duly compensated. I was now a real private investigator.

I left Frankie with the proprietor and the sleeping man on the floor and went forth to fight some more crime. The streets were wide, conjuring up an image of rushing cattle in the days of the Old West. By this time, Rusty was walking down the middle of the street with cars and pickups passing him by as if he were the personification of a yellow median stripe. What I'm trying to say is that he wasn't hard to follow.

The end of town in Sandy Creek came about abruptly – one minute I was strolling along and there was a little building on the left and a little building on the right, rinse, repeat, and the next minute, as far as the eye could see, only tan desert and Saguaro cacti. I'd been staying maybe three hundred feet behind Rusty. He seemed oblivious. The sun baked the asphalt, causing optical illusions of all kinds. First, I would have sworn the pavement was dancing up ahead – why, I had no clue. Then, I would have bet the farm, if I'd had one, that somehow a pond had formed between Rusty and me. But when I got there, it had evaporated. Arizona is weird.

A single-story adobe home with an almost equal-sized garage and probably workshop welcomed Rusty at the end of a short, unpaved spur off the main road. Man, it was hot! My 15 dollars of Evian in the car was probably boiling by this time. And could I ever go for some more iced tea! Some salty Fritos wouldn't hurt, either – pretty sure it'd be classified as health food now, even in Mary Ellen's book.

A bush of some kind near the trailer's corner made me feel I'd be well hidden, assuming someone wasn't searching very hard for a six-foot, two-hundred-pound minister in khakis, blue crew-knit shirt, white New Balance 624s, and a straw hat that in no way kept the sun off his burning scalp. I could hear voices inside, Rusty's for sure. The dwelling had a sizeable picture window in the middle. I wanted to take a gander but, of course, I couldn't just put my nose to the glass as if I was at an aquarium. Only way I could figure how to do it was to grab some of the sagebrush blowing around, hold it up by my face, and march by the window as if my job was to clear the desert of the stuff. And peek quickly in the window a time or two.

Jasmine was sitting at a table right in front of the window with a tissue to her eyes. That was peek one. Peek two revealed a nose blow and very red eyes. She was crying. Clues are definitely my thing.

Sure enough, upon my return I discovered the water in my car was too hot to drink, but a vending machine outside the Sandy Creek Taxi Service and Funeral Parlor ("You can ride with us now or later") rendered up a nice, cold Dr. Pepper. A sign pointed me to the Sandy Creek Marshal's Office. Turns out the marshal wasn't available, but the old fella with a cowboy hat behind the desk – a deputy, I presumed – said he'd be glad to take my complaint. Except I didn't have a complaint, just a clue. I began with the airplane and the hotel.

"You were having sex with her, weren't you, Mr. Burgess?"

I mean, come on people! Does everyone have sex on the brain? I finished my tale with my most recent observation.

"Mister," the deputy began, "I don't know about the laws up there in Massatwoshits, but down here we frown on voyeurism. I should put you in the pokey right now and hold you till the marshal comes back from lunch."

"First of all," I countered, "it's Connecticut, and second of all, it's 3 o'clock. What's the marshal doing still at lunch?"

"Marshal doesn't do well in the summers when everyone else is on Daylight Savings Time. It may be 3 o'clock here, but it's also 3 o'clock in LA, and 2 o'clock in Denver. Stuff like that throws him. But regardless, it's none of your nevermind. It so happens that I know the people you're talking about, Rusty and Jasmine. Ever-body has their ups and downs, their little fights, their little he-saids, she-saids, their little get-out-of-the-house-before-I-shoot-you-in-the-ass times. Rusty and Jasmine are good people, stay to themselves, don't bother nobody. He works at the filling station over there, and she's gone a lot. That's all I know, and that's all I care to know. I don't want to know ever-body's secrets, and I don't want ever-body to know I only take one bath a week. This is the West, Mr. Burgess, and I highly recommend you stick to minding your own business."

With the overpowering fragrance in the room now identified, I promised to do so and left. He'd pointed to a filling station kitty-corner to the marshal's office. As I was doing my best impression of John Wayne's walk while staring down a single gas pump and an air hose, Rusty turned a corner, no doubt returning to work from his own lunch. I bought another Dr. Pepper from the machine and jumped into my car. Too hot to walk to Jasmine's again.

But worse in a car whose windows had been left up. The air conditioner on high had no time and no chance to make a difference in the half mile to Jasmine's. I parked the Camry right in front of an ancient cactus that could've be dead for centuries, for all I knew. I rang the bell. I knocked loudly. A coyote-looking kind of dog ambled by and nodded his head. Or was it a dog-looking kind of coyote? I appreciated the greeting, nonetheless. I wondered if the door was locked – it was. I wondered if the back door was locked – it was. I wondered if I could find some more sagebrush. I couldn't. Knowing that Rusty wasn't home, however, emboldened me. I went to the large picture window and peered in. I saw no fish, but I did see Jasmine sprawled unconscious on the floor with a swollen, left-eye bruise in the making.

I considered calling 911, but I feared I might get either room service or Deputy B.O. I had no choice. A rock, the hard-to-believe remains of a long-ago glacial seabed, smashed easily through the glass on the back door. Reaching inside, I opened it. I had to get Jasmine out of there before Rusty came home. I wasn't prepared for the welcome blast of cold air nor for the cat that materialized from somewhere. The cat and I examined its mistress and were both glad to hear a lady-like snore. It occurred to me that I'd never lifted an adult before. First, I tried to cradle her in my arms like I used to do with our son, but Jasmine must have outweighed him by more than a hundred pounds, which was not so surprising since Matthew was maybe two at the time. That wasn't going to work. Then, kneeling on the floor beside her, I put her upper torso over my right shoulder, cradled my arms around her midsection and stood up. Or, tried to stand up. I was intending to try again when someone screamed in my ear, "What the hell are you doing?" The someone, of course, was Jasmine.

Needless to say, I was taken aback. As in the almost-losing-bowel-and-bladder-control kind of taken aback.

"Jasmine, are you okay?"

"Of course I'm okay. What are you doing here? How'd you get in? Where's Rusty? Why are you hugging me?"

I had to admit, I was starting to miss my church.

"You were unconscious. I was trying to get you out of here, to save you."

"You stupid moron," Jasmine said, quite judgmentally. "If Rusty comes home and sees you, he'll put you six feet under. Get out of here!"

"Jasmine, something funny is going on. It doesn't take a highly skilled dick to see that." I thought using a familiar term might bring back the nice Jasmine. "The fact is, I was robbed. Another fact is I got knocked out cold. Another fact is you told me Rusty was abusive to you.

So, young lady, I need you to tell me if you want to be saved or not."

"I want you to get out of here. Now! Look, I'll give you back your money, but you need to leave."

"And my MasterCard," I said.

"Here, take it."

"And my AARP card."

"Your what?"

"Never mind."

"Now please leave."

"So, what is it? Is Rusty abusive? Do you want me to bring the marshal?"

"No, it's just – it's complicated. You have to leave! I'll have to tell him how the window got smashed, and he's going to be furious. So leave, will you?"

As I drove through Sandy Creek, I saw Rusty at the filling station sitting in a chair under an awning with an electric fan in another chair, its wire stretched through an open window. That would be the life, wouldn't it? Sitting in 108-degree heat with an electric fan blowing 108-degree wind in your face. I had no doubt this was how all those skeletons were made.

***

The drive back to Tucson was uneventful. I'd worked up quite an appetite and still hadn't got my Fritos fix. A Circle K convenience store answered my prayers. They also have a way of cooking hot dogs on those rolling hot tube things. I sat in my air-conditioned car and ate gleefully while listening to ESPN radio on Sirius. The Yankees and Red Sox were tied for first in the division. This was where I'd failed Matt. I'd brought him up to be a good Yankees fan, but when I wasn't looking, he'd changed teams. I still don't know how that happened.

Back in my room, I couldn't wait to take a shower. Which reminded me, I had to pick up a shirt before the end of the week. That was, assuming the private eye class people would overlook my truancy.

I related the details of my day and plans to Mary Ellen, and, surprise, surprise – she thought I was nuts. "You come home immediately, Dickie. I can't be there to rescue you as I have for 30 years. You are in way over your head. And, by the way, what did you have to eat tonight?"

I hated to lie to Mary Ellen, but if I told the truth another reprimand would follow. "Salad," I said. "A nice garden salad with lots of radishes and peppers and broccoli and tomatoes. And some fish. A special Arizona fish."

"I never heard of an Arizona fish," she shot back.

"Well, they try to keep it a secret because otherwise people back east would buy them out, and the locals really love it."

I wasn't comfortable with how easy that came out, but I did admire it.

CHAPTER SIX

"Of course, Mr. Burgess, you're good to go," the school's registrar informed me the next morning. I'd driven around the block several times only to discover that my private eye college was holding its classes in a junior high school that was in recess for the summer. "We'll just have you complete a little quiz on 'clues,' which is what we studied yesterday. And don't worry, the answers are on the other side if you need some help."

I found a desk and chair. Question one: "You're on a case involving a famous politician who was found dead in an apartment. He was naked. The apartment belonged to a call girl. What was his name (hint: it rhymes with Dockefeller)?"

A. Richard Nixon.

B. Franklin D. Roosevelt

C. Dave Barry

D. Nelson Rockefeller

I didn't see a space for a write-in answer because except for the fact that he isn't dead, I would have sworn the answer was Bill Clinton.

Rockefeller, though, was hard to ignore. I checked the back: I was right!

The next four questions were much easier. I had passed "Clues." I was on my way.

After high-fiving me, the registrar directed me to the room where the rest of the class had already begun a lecture on "Following People." I found a seat in the back row and gave the instructor my undivided attention. Or tried to. Everyone else seemed to have a cup of coffee or tea or something, and several were stuffing their faces with donuts. I searched for the source. Up front was a table with mounds of pastries and urns of hot liquids. Proceeding as unobtrusively as I could, I made my way to the refreshments, and was in the middle of trying to load a third donut on my plate when the teacher addressed me: "Halt! You! The man with the donuts! Halt in the name of the law!"

I put the third donut back – it would've been hard to balance anyway given the tiny paper plate. "You mean me?" I asked.

"Yes, you. Put the donuts down – now! Let me see your hands – now! Come up here."

"You mean now?" I queried.

"Yes, now! Stand over there. Mister, were you following me?"

"Following you? Do you mean did I understand what you were saying? Because I have to confess I wasn't listening. I was so excited to see that you had maple-frosted donuts."

"I mean were you following me because my wife hired you because she thinks I'm cheating on her, which I may or may not be doing, but that's no concern of yours?"

After flapping my jaw noiselessly trying to think of something to say, it dawned on me: I was being used as a pawn in the presentation. I decided to play along. "You got me," I said. "You're way too good at this. I'm a beginner. What should I have done differently?"

"First of all, don't wear loud colors. Red is out, always out. You want to be forgettable. Don't want to be noticed. So no red shirts. Second of all, you caught my eye because you weren't sneaking. You were just walking. You've got to learn to sneak. We'll be offering a seminar after dinner called 'Sneaking Up on People' for an extra $100. Third of all, you aren't wearing a disguise. I could tell from way up here that you're a minister."

I couldn't believe it. "How'd you know that?" I said.

"You mean you really are a minister?" He was flummoxed. "Let's take a break."

I discovered that if I put my index finger through the hole of the third donut and held the cup of coffee with the rest of the fingers and thumb on my right hand, I could easily balance the other two donuts on their little bitty paper plate with my left.

"You've got crumbs on your front," said the man, who was wearing a nametag that announced "Hello my name is Jim Bob."

"Oh, thanks," I replied, wishing I had a free hand to sweep them off.

"You did real good up there. He almost didn't see you sneaking up on him."

"I wasn't sneaking up on him. I was just going for the snacks."

"You lie good, too. You may be able to test out of *that* class."

Lunch was cold cuts, chips, and the remainder of the pastries. I'd gotten my money's worth so far. Afterwards, we broke up into groups of four and were told to go outside and follow each other. Much confusion ensued. Everyone wanted to be the follower, no one wanted to be the one followed. I learned one team had a fistfight. Our team eventually settled on my idea of taking turns, which the others thought was ingenious. I was rewarded with the dubious honor of "perpetrator-on-the-run." After an hour sitting under a lone oak tree on the quadrangle, I could only conclude I'd slipped my captors' pursuit. When I returned to the classroom, no one was there. I decided to head back to the hotel. I'd skip their dinner and seminar on sneaking. I was beginning to wonder what kind of education I'd signed up for.

I called my friend Chief Blaney of the Hillsdale Police Department. "I think you must have made a mistake, Bob," I said. "I can't believe this class will qualify me to be a private investigator. I've never met so many dumb people in all my life, although I will say the donuts have been terrific."

"Richard," he said, "Police work is not all cops and robbers, *LA Law, Law and Order, NCIS, NCIS Miami, Criminal Minds, Magnum PI, Columbo, NYPD, Hawaii Five-O*, not to mention *Cops* and *Cops Reloaded* stuff. Generally, at least in Hillsdale, it's doing boring things and trying to stay awake. Don't worry. When you get back, I'll fill in the missing pieces and then send you over to work out an arrangement with Myron. He's been in the business a long time – former cop, all that. A couple of years with him and you can hang up your own shingle."

Sounded good to me. I couldn't wait.

***

The rest of the week went mostly like the first couple of days except for squeezing in a trip to Dillard's for a shirt. There was a class on "Stakeouts" that covered how to sit in your car waiting for someone to come out of their house before they went wherever they were going. After which, of course, we would employ the skill of following people that we'd already got down pat. One of the problems with stakeouts, the instructor said, was when you had to go to the bathroom. You couldn't very well up and drive to a McDonald's and use their toilet. From underneath his lectern, the instructor pulled out a Coke bottle. I was worried he was going to demonstrate but he didn't. I also wondered about his anatomy. One of the few women students asked what they should use. Again, he held up the Coke bottle. I wasn't getting something here. The woman raised her hand again but he ignored her.

Another class was on lock picking, and we got our own lock-picking kits. Still another was how to speak with a foreign accent when undercover. He recommended Spanish. A guy named Arturo raised his hand and inquired what language he should use. The teacher got that flummoxed stare again, and we enjoyed a break.

The morning class on Friday had to do with disguises. It was like using a foreign accent except this was visible, he said. The class nodded in silent admiration for the profundity of what they'd just learned.

"Wigs. Wigs and beards. You can't go wrong with wigs and beards."

I think it was the same woman with the Coke bottle issue who raised her hand. "What if you're a woman. Would you still wear a beard?" We took a break.

CHAPTER SEVEN

The instructor didn't show for the Friday afternoon session so we watched an old *Matlock* episode on video. That Andy Griffith was really something. Though I missed Opie. Around three, the registrar who, as it turns out, was also the Dean and President of "So You Want to Be a Private Investigator" College, mounted the stage in the room and called us forward one by one for our diplomas. Since he began with a guy named Allen, went to Bennett and on to Carlyle before concluding with a woman named Zernial, I worried that the omission of my name had to do with me taking more than my share of donuts. I needn't have given it a second thought.

"Ladies and gentlemen," Dean President Boros said into the microphone, "I am proud to announce the winner of this year's 'Most Likely to Succeed as a Private Investigator Award.' Richard Burgess, will you please come forward for your diploma and a special prize." The only time I'd received a standing ovation was when I wound down a sermon on "The

Mystery of the Holy Trinity" after 50 minutes with the words, "In conclusion…." I wasn't sure how to act. Dean President Boros had tears in his eyes as he handed me a vinyl-covered folder with a certificate in it that had my name misspelled with but one "s." Since each of us had paid close to two thousand dollars for this course, I found myself dreaming that maybe a lot of that money had gone into the special prize I was about to receive.

Dean President Boros asked his assistant, Sanford, who was a dead ringer for the guy I saw every morning in the restroom peeking over his closed stall door, to "now play the music!" He had to ask again. And again. Then, so loudly that most everyone fell to the floor and crawled under tables, we heard the beginning of the *Dragnet* theme – "dum-de-dum-dum." "The next track, for crying out loud," Dean President Boros bellowed. I couldn't be sure, but this one sure sounded like a lot of heavy breathing and sighs and moans. Finally, he asked Sanford to shut it down. Without further ado, he directed our attention to the heavy velvet curtains behind us on the stage.

A new car? I wondered. A large travel poster of somewhere exotic and a model beside it holding a ticket like on *The Price is Right*?

"Richard, and say, may I call you Dick?"

"No, I'd rather you not," I said.

"Dick, we have a gift for you that you'll treasure forever. Open the curtain, Sanford!"

You wouldn't believe me if I told you the curtains actually parted. This is to say, he had to ask two more times.

Behind them was a small table with something on it. I glanced at Dean President Boros to see if he was as surprised as I was at the size of the prize. He didn't seem to be. With tears returning, he picked up a box containing a pair of cuff links with the seal of the college on them. "Dick, of course we couldn't get the whole name of our college on the cuff links, but we do have our initials, half on one and half on the other. I'm sure you'll wear them proudly as an alum of SYWTBAPI College."

Another standing ovation followed. Then a man in a green uniform appeared from stage right saying the rental period was up and everyone should leave the premises. "Post haste," I think he said. An educated sort of custodian.

I was accustomed to standing at the rear of church sanctuaries following services so people could shake my hand and lie to my face about my sermons. But when I got to the back of the classroom, everyone had cleared out. Must have had planes to catch.

CHAPTER EIGHT

I was so happy to be heading home I didn't mind the mental gymnastics I had to negotiate in making sure I wouldn't oversleep for my 7 AM flight back to Hartford, though Deputy B.O. mentioning L.A. did confuse me for a bit. I'd thought a lot about Jasmine and Rusty. One minute I had no doubt it had been a simple setup and robbery; the next I was certain it was honest fear on Jasmine's face when she barged into my room. No one could be that good of an actor. She'd said it was complicated. Using skills I might have learned in my "Clues" class, had there been anything to learn, I had a feeling that "complicated" meant it was a little of this and a little of that – a little of robbery and a little of scared witless. But there was nothing I could do about it now. She'd ordered me to stay out of her life, and at that point, I didn't have a better idea. My plan was to go home, take Mary Ellen out for dinner, make contact with Myron, my PI supervisor, and get on with the next step of being "Richard Burgess, Private Investigator."

I'd forgotten to phone in 24 hours in advance to secure a place in either section A or B for my Southwest flight, so I chose a middle seat between a man and a woman. Turned out they were married. I offered to let them sit next to each other, but they said they preferred to sit where they were. Not that that kept them from steady chit-chat for the five-hour flight home. Sometimes I leaned back so they could see each other when talking, and sometimes I leaned forward. The man seemed to like to speak from the front edge of his seat, while his wife, the larger one of the two, preferred to speak behind my back. When we landed in Hartford, I was exhausted. But at least the pretzels were good.

Because my married friends and I had been in the rear of the plane, we were among the last to exit. Located midway between Hartford and Springfield, Massachusetts, Bradley International is a small airport called "International" because they have one flight a day to Toronto. But what it lacks in size, it makes up in convenience. Normally, at least in my experience, it's not crowded. That Saturday, though, was different. I could barely make my way through the throng of people standing in their sections A and B ready to board, clogging the path of the deplaning souls. It always happens: one person gets nervous that their number won't be honored so they go stand in line and are quickly surrounded by others fearful that somehow they're going to be left behind.

I'd stopped to apologize for rolling my carry-on over someone's foot when a voice caught my attention. Familiar, but not Connecticut-familiar. Then a laugh. Again familiar. Although I couldn't see the person who'd been emitting the voice and laugh, I had her location pegged. At the rear of the B section standees.

Walking in that direction, I heard, "and where will you be staying?"

And Where Will You Be Staying?

(Part Two)

If Elvis had tapped me on the shoulder and begun singing "Love Me Tender," I couldn't have been as stunned as I was seeing Jasmine in Hartford awaiting a flight to somewhere. My knees went limp while at the same time my body weighed 300 pounds. I stumbled to a chair in the airport gateway.

I thought Jasmine was out of my life, a relatively brief, though educational, interlude in my quest for certification as a private investigator. I had last seen her five days ago in Arizona when she told me to beat it before Rusty came home. And now, here she was – waiting to board a plane two thousand miles away. Believe me, it would have been easier to wrap my head around Elvis.

The only person seated in the entire boarding area happened to be across from me. "I refuse to stand, also," declared the woman in jeans, baseball cap, and neckerchief. "These dopes who're standing make a mockery of Southwest's perfect system. Jump in at the last minute, I always say."

"Yeah, jump in at the last minute, that's what I always say, too," I replied, still in shock, my eyes burning into Jasmine's back some fifteen feet in front of me.

"You're white as a sheet," she said. "Must be going to Tucson for some sun."

"This plane is going back to Tucson?" I asked.

"You mean you're getting on a plane and don't know where it's going? Are you well?"

I had to walk. And I had to claim my luggage downstairs. And then I had to buy a ticket to Tucson.

I called Mary Ellen as I raced down the steps. Got the answering machine. My voice: "You've reached the Burgess residence. If this is a pastoral emergency please call Rev. Burgess's cell" followed by my mobile number.

Couldn't believe I hadn't thought to change that.

I left a message. "Hi honey, uh, you'll never guess what happened. I have to go back to Tucson. Long story. I'll catch up with you later. It's a beautiful day, isn't it! Love you. Bye."

I reached the carousel surrounded by more people than possibly could have been on our airplane. And not a single bag in sight.

I couldn't wait. My recently purchased purple Samsonite Spin Trunk would just have to keep spinning around and around.

I raced back up the stairs and headed to the Southwest check-in area. No one was in line – which was good – but no one was behind the counter, either. I was searching for a little bell to summon attention when a ticket agent appeared as if from heaven. "May I help you?"

"Yes, you have a flight leaving for Tucson any minute. I need a ticket."

"You're in luck. The flight is delayed because they have to swap out the cookies for crackers since they noticed the "consume by" date on the cookies expired two years ago. Won't be leaving for another half hour."

I would definitely be boarding last, I realized, which meant I'd be walking down the aisle facing Jasmine regardless of where she was sitting. Putting my SYWTBAPI College training to use, I realized I needed a disguise.

Airport CNBC shops are vastly underrated. There isn't much any desperate traveler might need that they don't have. Even wigs. Right there on the rotating display with ties and belts and umbrellas were a couple of women's wigs. No beards, though. One wig was a long gray one; the other was shoe polish black with tight curls. Easy decision – $19.99 wasn't a bad price, I didn't think, for a black wig. I'd been cursed or blessed, depending on your point of view, with nothing more than peach fuzz since puberty. I'd bought my share of razors and gone through the motions from time to time, but usually for an excuse to present a "just shaved" smell to the world. I also picked up a plastic police badge from the toy carousel. The SYWTBAPI teacher had said such a thing could come in handy if we flashed it fast enough. We had practiced on each other, and I was the clear champion. Likely, that was what earned me the cuff links.

I'd never held a wig before, let alone put one on my head. Plus, all things considered, I would've preferred some privacy to a busy airport men's room, but you work with what you've got and ignore people who fall down laughing on a urine-soiled floor.

The deal was, I wasn't sure which was front or back. Or side, for that matter. There wasn't a tag inside to indicate the correct way to affix it to one's head. I cocked it high on my head; I cocked it low on my brow. I pitched it like a beret first to the right, then to the left. Finally, I yanked it straight down, grateful that the elastic seemed heavy-duty.

Once again, Jasmine had chosen an aisle seat about midway back next to the "stooge," a term I'd learned at college for "man about to be taken advantage of by a femme fatale." The aisle seat behind her was available. With my head down, leading with my wig, I aimed for it.

The overhead bins were nearly full, but there seemed to be room enough for my carry-on if I could just readjust a piece or two.

"Excuse me, madam, may I assist you?" It was a flight attendant. And, yes, she was talking to me. With a shove, she and I managed to complete my mission and I said hello to my seatmate, an attractive young woman – college student, I surmised – who didn't seem any too pleased to be sitting with a large older woman – or man.

I pulled my wig downward almost to my eyebrows, put my head back and closed my eyes. I had some serious thinking to do.

This impulsive streak I was on was new. I could see myself telling a therapist about it and being assured it was nothing serious, nothing medication couldn't help. As you may have noticed, I do care about people and I've always been curious. And, not least, I did love my Spenser. So put all that together with a delayed midlife crisis and voila! You have an absolute idiot.

But it was too late to seek professional help. Somehow, I had to warn the man in front of me. And also, even though I knew what Mary Ellen would say, I wasn't entirely convinced Jasmine was willingly playing the role of "pigeon" – another term I'd learned: a woman who sets up a stooge. I just couldn't erase from my mind the panic on her face in my hotel room right before Rusty knocked my block off: it was sheer terror, the likes of which I hadn't beheld since the shower scene in *Psycho*.

Because the engines were so loud, I couldn't make out much of the conversation between Jasmine and the stooge. Every now and then, she'd laugh that laugh of hers that I'd first heard in connection with the ketchup on my shirt. He seemed charmed and charming. And, I'd say, expensively dressed.

I eventually gave up trying to listen in, flipped down my tray table, secured my wig, put my head down, and slept through the meal of crackers. I woke up when the student next to me jabbed me in the side. "What?" I nearly shouted.

"They said to put your tray table in the upright position. And, pardon me, but I've got to say, that's the ugliest wig I've ever seen. And given how you were snoring, I'm pretty sure you're a man. That plus the ketchup stain I see now. So, eew. That's all I've got to say: Eew!"

A month ago, I would have invited her to my church when she was in Connecticut. I couldn't see how that would be helpful now, though.

After landing, I determined to keep Jasmine and her friend in my view. This time, however, trying to wriggle my bag out from up top, I was aided by a man probably twenty years older than I. When he handed it to me, he winked. I hoped my college friend noticed.

CHAPTER TWO

Jasmine and Mr. Stooge preceded me down the aisle and into the terminal. He appeared to be about my height and stature, which is former athlete gone to pot. Jasmine must not have had any baggage to claim because they parted company. She headed outdoors into the desert heat, and he aimed for the baggage merry-go-round.

Outside, he crossed the first roadway and hailed a local cab from the next curb. I did the same. "Follow that cab," I said. The driver turned around and said, "You've got to be kidding. Nobody says 'follow that cab' except in the movies."

I realized I wasn't commanding the sort of respect I'd come to expect, so I removed my wig – Rev. Burgess, at your service. Again, I implored, "I'm not kidding. There's an extra five in it for you if you keep up with that cab." It was all I could do to convince him I was on the up and up, and, by the time I did, the first cab had been lost to the circumferential road around the airport. I told him to head out anyway. A yellow cab in a sea of yellow cabs, I know, but thanks to some fast driving, we soon came upon the stooge and settled in behind him. We drove and drove. And drove some more. From time to time, I'd remind the driver to drop back a few cars so we wouldn't be so obvious. Learned that in school. Or was it from Spenser? Eventually we came to a motel, the Scorpion Inn. No wonder there wasn't airport pickup.

I asked the driver to take a spin around the block. Which took about half an hour. Fact is, there aren't any regular kind of blocks that far out in the desert.

The fare was $87.50. I gave the driver a crisp $100 bill, thought about saying, "Keep the change," but ended up asking for $5 back, thanking him for his good following work. Really bad words came from his mouth. Really bad words.

I didn't know the name of the victim-in-waiting, so I couldn't simply ask for his room number. I pulled on the wig and pushed through the front door of the Scorpion Inn.

"Yes, may I help you, madam… sir… friend?" the man at the desk said, a quizzical expression spreading on his face with each guess.

"Yes," I said in what I considered a decent falsetto. "My husband just checked in without me. Can you tell me what room he's in?"

"That must be Mr. Honey. He's in 107, to your right as you exit."

"Thank you very much," I said, turning to leave.

"But, madam, I have to tell you, Mr. Honey isn't married. So don't pull that stunt on me, okay?"

I tossed my head back in obvious insult, almost losing my wig, and walked out in a proper huff. And headed to Room 107.

The Scorpion Inn is a single-story line of rooms in concrete-block décor because it's all concrete blocks. Two metal chairs sat in front of each room's window. A little table – must have come with the chairs – sat in between. An ashtray perched on every table reminded me of my former smoking days. The twilight hours didn't help the beauty of the place, although why someone would choose desert camouflage for a color escaped me. Clearly, whatever profit the motel made had gone into their humongous blinking sign ("Rooms by the year, month, day or hour; hot tubs, vibrating beds"). Bursts of the multi-colored lights illuminated my path as I counted down from Room 125 to

Room 107. I checked my memory for a lecture on "How to Tell Someone They're Being Played for a Stooge," but couldn't remember that being covered. So I knocked.

"You're the ugliest woman I've ever seen!" a naked Mr. Honey exclaimed. "And why are you wearing men's clothes? But, hey, it works for me, come on in."

I stepped in, fearing the slime of the place might infect my shoes. I had seriously overestimated Mr. Honey. Apparently not every person who dresses well has good taste in all matters.

"Sir," I said. "I've come here to tell you that you're about to be hurt."

"That works for me, too," he said. "Let's get it on."

"No, no. I'm serious. I'm not going to hurt you, but that woman you sat next to on the plane is."

"You mean a threesome? Wow! Do you work for a great agency or what!"

"Sir, would you please put some clothes on. This is awkward."

"Sure thing. I bet you like to tear 'em off, am I right or am I right?"

"Look, that woman and her husband or boyfriend or whatever are going to come and beat you up and steal your money. I've traveled all the way from Hartford to warn you. Whatever you do, don't answer the door in the middle of the night." There, I'd said it. Mission accomplished.

I'd turned to leave when Mr. Honey grabbed my left arm and spun me around. My wannabe lover's face was now no more than a couple of inches from mine, his eyes closed and his lips puckered so tightly I thought they might squeal. Instinctively, I employed a move I'd only read about: I kneed him in the groin, and ran out of the room.

Did you know that Udriveme Rent-A-Car will bring you a car no matter where you are? I knew this because I'd been a proud Udriveme customer since forever. I called them from my hiding place behind an old Willys Jeep a few hundred feet down the road from the Scorpion Inn. They asked my location. "I'll be standing on the highway right before you come to the Scorpion Inn," I said. "I'll be waving a black curly wig."

Mary Ellen hadn't called. That concerned me. Our 25-year marriage hadn't had a single major fight. Of course, there had been more than a few protracted silences so I feared this was another. In five minutes, though, I would have prayed for protracted silence. I dialed.

"Dickie," she said with a measured calm that could only mean she'd been talking with her sister, the psychologist. "I have to accept that you are an adult, which, as you know, is sometimes very hard for me to do. As an adult, you have the right to ruin your life if you want to. You also have the right not to be concerned about what people will think of you when you turn up on the evening news. I think as religious people we should say our prayers. And pray that the Lord should take one of us so the other can be happy. And then I can go live with my sister." And she hung up. Of course she did.

I didn't have a sister. Or a brother, for that matter. Sibling dynamics were something I just didn't get. But, I was pretty sure that although it had been Mary Ellen's voice I'd just heard, she was, in fact, channeling her sister, whom her folks had written out of their will, for good reason, as far as I could tell. Whatever – I couldn't do anything about it now. I decided I'd head back towards Tucson, stop at the first shopping mall I came to, and buy some clothes and a suitcase. That should put me back at the beautiful Scorpion Inn some time before midnight, where I would stake out Room 107 and await Jasmine and Rusty. Given the desert flora and fauna, I wouldn't even need a Coke bottle.

CHAPTER THREE

I had to drop the Udriveme man in Green Valley, which was a blessing because, lo and behold, their office was in a mall that had an outlet store: "More Brands, More Savings." I bought five of everything I would need, plus a couple of dresses and another Samsonite bag like the one still spinning in Hartford. Instead of purple, this one was lime green – the stuff at outlet malls is there for a reason. At the CVS across the lot, I purchased toiletries including a bag of ladies' razors because – well, you never know.

I hadn't thought to eat since breakfast, which meant that either I was sick or dead or had had my life turned upside down. I didn't feel sick, didn't feel dead. So, there you go.

After securing my newest possessions in the trunk of another Udriveme Camry, I chose a Golden Corral restaurant over a McDonald's. There was a guy who did a documentary some time ago about eating McDonald's every meal for a year. Yes, he gained weight. Yes, he was not healthy at the end. Yes, he would smell like a fry bin for the rest of his life. Yes, McDonald's sued him for some reason. But still, I envied him. That's how much I love McDonald's.

So, why choose the Golden Corral? Because it was "All you can eat – $5.99," that's why. Remember, I'm cheap in a Yankee way.

All I could eat apparently qualified me for special attention. A nice young woman manager in a cowboy hat, short skirt, red pigtails, and high heels sidled up to me and said, "Shouldn't we let others have a turn?" I was full anyway and had spotted a Circle K on the drive between the Scorpion Inn and Green Valley that would suffice in case I needed to top things off. So I was fine with her suggestion.

I retraced my steps and found the motel without any trouble but noticed a red pickup in front of Room 107 that hadn't been there before. It could, of course, be the tenant in Room 109 or 105 aiming badly. But, if I'd had time to worry I was too late, I shouldn't have – I was too late. Rusty and Jasmine were beating a hasty retreat to the red pickup.

Since I knew where they lived, I didn't feel compelled to race after them. I'd get there soon enough. So I left the car running in front of the office entrance, went in (sans wig, of course), flashed my junior police badge, and told the clerk I was responding to a robbery in Room 107, and could he please call it in; I had to follow the perpetrators.

Turned out that Rusty and Jasmine weren't rushing back to Sandy Creek, either, since I easily caught up to them on I-10 out of Tucson and we settled in on an 80-miles-per-hour pace along with everyone else. I was doing my "drop back, speed up every now and then" routine when upon accelerating to regain my favored position two hundred feet behind my target, I heard a siren and spotted beautiful red and blue lights glimmering in the otherwise pitch black night in my rear-view mirror. Naturally, I assumed the sheriff's car was on its way to a donut shop, so I slowed and edged over a bit on the shoulder. Imagine my surprise when the car didn't pass.

"Do you know how fast you were going, Mr. Burgess?" said the portly sheriff in his fifties while closely examining my license. "We have laws out here in Arizona, even if you don't up there in Connecticut. And where's that exactly? Near Massatwoshits?"

I'd been given a question, a statement, and another question. And now the flashlight beamed its one-thousand-watt bulb into my eyes.

"Sixty-five on the nose," I lied, "and, yes, Connecticut borders Massachusetts. The reason I'm hurrying is because I've just witnessed a robbery and probable assault and battery and I'm trying to catch up to the assailants, the perpetrators, the bad guys."

"Do you know who the aforementioned assailants, perpetrators, bad guys are?"

"As a matter of fact I do. First names are Rusty and Jasmine. They live in Sandy Creek."

"I know them," he said. "They're good people. Salt of the earth. They wouldn't hurt a fly. He has an important job at the filling station. I don't know what you're up to, mister, but I'm going to need you to step out of the car. And keep your hands where I can see them."

The sheriff directed me to the front of my car and ordered me to lean over and place my hands on the hood. I did so. For a half second or less. The metal was scorching hot, and without thinking, I pulled back with all the haste that goes with the word "yeouch!" and accidently, honestly, hit the man in the face with my left elbow. He was now down on the ground on hands and knees crying, "My contacts! I can't see without my contacts!"

As a pastor, I'd never ignored a crying person. But there's a first time for everything.

I knew from my reading of mysteries that it would be only a matter of time before a BOLO – that's Be On the Lookout – would be broadcast for me and my car. So, after making it successfully to Sandy Creek, I searched for a place to hide the Camry. And found it – behind the Sandy Creek Taxi Service and Funeral Parlor in an unoccupied garage bay. I didn't see a hearse so I figured they must be on a call of one kind or another and would be back. But for now, it seemed the best place to park. I grabbed my lime green Samsonite Spin Trunk and headed off to find a place to stay. To cover my bets, I called Udriveme and left a message saying my car had been stolen. That I'd be in touch about a replacement. Spenser would do something like that, I had no doubt.

The Sandy Creek Wild West Hotel and Computer Repair seemed inviting, what with their open door and a man shouting, "You lookin' for a room, mister? Computer crash on ya?" Despite having just reported my car stolen, I didn't want to bandy my name around. So I asked if I could pay cash instead of using a credit card. "Yes," he said, "but you have to pay in advance." I told him that wouldn't be a problem, and paid for a week – who knows? – using ten of my twenty-dollar bills.

The bed was comfortable, the plumbing worked – what more could I ask? I called Mary Ellen knowing she wouldn't answer and left a message telling her I loved her and hoped to be home in a few days. I could only hope she'd be there.

Although it was open for breakfast, I didn't feel comfortable returning to the Double R Bar Saloon and Chinese Restaurant for fear of being recognized, so instead I chose a competitor down the way, Deanna's Dinky Diner. Deanna didn't seem to have diversified into a complimentary line of work like other places, but that was okay.

I ordered a Southwestern omelet, home fries, toast, and coffee. I wanted to ask for some pancakes on the side, but to tell the truth, last night's binge at the Golden Corral was still in the process of digestion.

"We're supposed to be on the lookout for a white Camry." That from Deanna, I gathered, who was talking to a man at the counter in shorts and a T-shirt that read, "My dog is smarter than your honor roll kid." "Said he's six foot tall and from up north."

I wheeled my Spin Trunk into the men's restroom with a handsomely printed sign over the toilet, "My aim is to please, so please watch your aim." After donning the wig, I returned to the dining area.

"I would have sworn you was a man," Deanna said placing my order in front of me. "I don't usually get those things wrong."

"Well," I said, "no offense taken."

CHAPTER FOUR

If someone were to interview me about my first days as a private investigator operating without a license, I would, of course, be arrested for my plastic police badge flashing. But assuming that could be overlooked, I would want to tell my interviewer how hard it is to turn gut instincts into actual strategies. Case in point: I was feeling an inner tug to revisit Rusty and Jasmine's house. Can't explain it – I just did. As to what I thought I might find? I had no idea.

The weather in Sandy Creek hadn't changed much in a few days. I ditched the wig in a trash receptacle and headed for Rusty and Jasmine's. Hot? Oh, my! Sweat? Not so much – the highly touted "dry heat" meant the evaporation of water was virtually instantaneous. Such, of course, wasn't always a good thing.

I couldn't tell if anyone was home. I'd noticed that Rusty's filling station had no business when I passed, and he wasn't sitting out front enjoying hot air blowing in his face.

Could have been in the back attending to vital matters in the important job the sheriff had been referring to, I supposed. The large detached garage and workshop in the rear of the lot I'd noted before beckoned me. Peering through a side window, I saw the red pickup and a Prius. A Prius? Rusty and Jasmine didn't seem the Prius types. I was in the process of upgrading my opinions of them when an arm was unceremoniously thrust around my neck and I was hugged dearly to someone.

"What are you doing here?" It was Rusty, his voice having been indelibly seared into my memory from when he made fun of my tighty-whities. "Ain't I seen you somewhere before?"

"I'm sorry to bother you," I said, still being held from the back in such a way that prohibited anything resembling a face-to-face conversation, "but have you considered where you'll spend eternity?"

"You're that preacher man. I knew you was familiar. Well, reverend, you've just bought yourself a peck of trouble. Jasmine, come out here, we've got company!"

Now, here's where schooling for PIs pays off in spades. Once again, I observed the look on Jasmine's face to be out of character for the situation. She appeared simultaneously horrified and a tad sympathetic. The kind of person who'd prefer a Prius, perhaps. I had little time to admire my detecting abilities, however, as between the two of them they succeeded in binding my legs and hands with rope. For good measure, a rag that smelled oddly of deep-fried something was stuffed in my mouth. My stomach growled in anticipation.

I was placed somewhat roughly into the back of the pickup, and a tarp was thrown over me. Following a short, bumpy ride, they hauled me out and deposited me in a self-storage unit. Before the overhead sliding door was closed and locked, I saw a sign by the entrance boasting "Desert Heights Self-Storage – Air-Conditioned Bins Available." That gave me hope. But it needn't have – someone apparently forgot to pay the electrical.

How I longed for 108-degree air. I'd even more than welcomed a fan blowing 108-degree air. I'd gotten through a college science requirement by taking "Biology for Nurses" instead of the regular 101 course because everyone said it was easier. Hard to prove by me – I barely passed. What I did remember, however, was that a human biological specimen couldn't last long inside an oven baking in the desert heat.

Jasmine had been the one who tied my hands, and she'd done it poorly. Was that on purpose? In any event, it wasn't hard to free my hands and then my feet. Whoopee. Now I could dance around before I died – this confirmed by a tug on the garage-type door that remained locked from the outside. Why there wasn't an emergency release on the inside was an issue I'd have to take up with management.

Thank God, I still had my cell phone. But, no thanks to my higher power, the battery was dead. Dead seemed to be a word that was filling my every thought. In case I needed amusement before I went the way of all flesh, I discovered I could play a game: "Guess the names of the animals whose bones now lie all around your feet." I ruled out javelinas and mountain lions. These were much smaller. I soon lost interest – maybe another time. My other companions in the sixteen-foot by twelve-foot space were boxes. Gaps around the rolling door provided enough light that I could make out logos of familiar companies whose shipping cartons had once delivered long-anticipated goods – Amazon, Staples, for example, plus several boasting the name of "Armbruster's Specialty Papers and Inks – since 1906." A large Staples box caught my eye: "ESPN" had been written in magic marker on the top.

Inside were dozens of envelopes with a return address of ESPN, ESPN Plaza, 700 Birch Street, Bristol, CT 06010. Each envelope contained a single five-by-seven piece of paper, surely torn from a pad, with an imprint in the top left, "From the Desk of Guy O'Neal." I knew O'Neal to be the famous ESPN interviewer whose weekly show, shot on location from places all over the globe, had won Emmys every year since its inception. It wasn't something I watched, as a rule, because, frankly, if the sport wasn't football, baseball, or basketball, I couldn't care less. O'Neal's shtick was to search out and highlight little known athletes who were the equivalent of American superstars in other countries – the smaller the country, the better. Since few of them played baseball or basketball, I often changed the channel when it came on. An all-star bocce player in Tajikistan may be a big deal for some people but not for me.

Each of the letters seemed similar. For example, "Dear R&J, 20 of product." The rest of the page or pages contained names followed by a country for each. It was always the same country for each set of names per letter. They were all signed, "Yours in sports, Guy." Postmarks dated back to December of last year.

If I'd known what "product" was I'd have been golden. However, this much seemed certain to this PI: Guy O'Neal and R and J were up to something they didn't want to name. Which might also explain why they were communicating the old-fashioned way rather than by email – emails remain forever. Letters, however, can be disposed of whenever one wants. Along with the carcasses of small animals and ministers. I was positive about two things: I was on to something, and I was going to die.

The walls of my cage were like the door: steel. Thin-gauge steel, but still steel and not balsa wood. I shouted for help for about ten minutes before deciding to preserve my energy. For what, I didn't know.

With delirium in my near future, I began hearing things. Like a gunshot. And I began seeing things. Like the garage door opening. And a man about six-and-a-half-feet tall with a gun in his hand and a pocket protector with pens in it.

"You look like you need some help," the angel apparition said.

"Yes," I replied, "and I'm sorry for all my sins, especially for when I fudged the attendance numbers in my report to the bishop."

"I don't get it, but then I don't get white man most of the time. My name is Arnold Bowman. I'm the father of the boy whose life you saved at the restaurant. I owe you big time."

Once, Mary Ellen and I drank a whole bottle of funeral home wine, so named because one of the local funeral homes always gave bottles of wine to the clergy in town at Christmas. The implicit quid pro quo: send us your dead people and we'll give you a bottle of cheap wine at Christmas. At the time, it had seemed like a fair deal. So, anyway, the bottle came a couple of days before Christmas, and one thing led to another, and since neither of us were good drinkers, we were quite tipsy in no time. That is, Mary Ellen was tipsy; I passed out. And I had a dream that now seeing the Native American in front of me brought to mind. I dreamed that I was in the company of all my childhood television heroes. There was Superman and Roy Rogers and Hopalong

Cassidy and Sergeant Friday. And there was Geronimo. And I was standing in front of Geronimo saying, "You'll have to go through me to take him." And the superheroes were backing away. Hopalong, in fact, spun around and ran. Sergeant Friday just stood there, stupefied. I wondered if this was my reward.

Arnold handed me a blessedly cold bottle of Poland Spring. And another. I can't possibly tell you how happy I was.

"Is your name really Arnold?" I asked. "Because if it is, it's a beautiful name, but I have to say you don't look like an Arnold."

"My parents named me after Arnold Schwarzenegger. Before he became governor. You may call me Eagle."

Okay, I knew at that point I was definitely dreaming. I'd envied Spenser for having a tough dude named Hawk who often came to his assistance. And now an Eagle had turned up in my dream. But I wasn't dreaming.

"But how did you know I was in trouble? Were you following me?"

"Yes and no," Eagle answered. "Frankie and I have an apartment above the Southwest Boots and Bolos across from the filling station where Rusty works. Saw you walking down the street looking like a Yankee in a broiler oven. Where'd you get that useless hat, anyway? And white sneakers? Wondered if you were the dude that Frankie told me about. Decided to trail you but had to finish my sandwich. Got to Rusty's just as his pickup was leaving. Looked around his property, didn't see you so figured you must have been in the back. Didn't know where you guys went, but drove around and got lucky when I saw Rusty and Jasmine leaving the storage place. Took me a while to locate you. Did you know when you yell 'help' you sound like a girl?"

I didn't care what I sounded like. My life had passed before my eyes and I'd come out on the plus side. On the drive back to Sandy Creek, Eagle told me he taught engineering at the local community college. Said he was the first in his family to graduate from college and was finishing his master's degree at the University of Arizona. He dropped me off at a Subway on the outskirts of Sandy Creek. "You saved my kid. I'll never forget you. Hope we meet again, but lose the hat, sneakers, and those pants, too, for that matter."

I'd love to tell you that he rode off on a white horse in a cloud of dust, but although there was plenty of dust that followed him, a ten-year-old black Corvette is nothing like a horse.

CHAPTER FIVE

The Subway foot-long special was good as always. Good, not great. Good, not bad. Just good, you know? The large bag of Fritos was better. Not to mention the bottles of Diet Coke. "I've always been curious," declared the young man at the cash register as I was tossing away the paper remains of my meal, "why do people order lots of food, really fattening stuff, and then order a Diet Coke?"

"I can't speak for others, of course," I began, "but some of us have discipline."

I wasn't surprised to discover that my Camry was no longer in the shed behind the taxi and funeral parlor company. After all, even the sorts of law enforcement personnel I'd encountered so far in Arizona should've been able to locate a vehicle involved in a crime within 24 hours if it had to be moved to park a hearse in a garage. My suitcase hadn't accompanied me to the almost death chamber, so I no longer had my wig, either. No car, no suitcase, no wig. Just me. And a thought.

I walked back in the Subway and found the snarky teenager picking olives out of the display case and popping them into his mouth. "Say," I said, "is that handsome 1990 or so Oldsmobile out there yours?"

"Yeah, what of it?"

"Well, I was wondering if when you get off work you could give me a lift up to Benson. I'll give you $50 up front."

"Sure, I can do that, mister," he said. "I'm through in an hour."

I spent the hour reading a copy of the daily Tucson paper someone had left behind. The Red Sox had swept the Yankees over the weekend and now held first place alone. Matthew would be happy. Maybe I'd phone and congratulate him. Would be nice to hear his voice.

Benson wasn't far away, and I-10 ran through it. I figured if I could get up there and stand by an on-ramp, some trucker, having refueled his rig in town, would be tickled pink to give me a ride to the Tucson airport exit.

My plan was working perfectly. The kid had discharged me by a Circle K; I'd loaded up on snacks and had just taken my place at the intersection of stoplight and on-ramp to I-10 and Tucson. I was mentally practicing which thumb to use when an Alamo County sheriff's car flipped on its lights, whooped its siren and pulled to the curb. My first instinct was to run, but I would have had to drop my bag of goodies lest the soda be shaken up and explode as I bounded over hill and dale. I'm just messing with you: running never occurred to me. Soiling my pants, however, did: It was the sheriff from yesterday.

"Hey, mister. Don't you know it's against the law to hitchhike? Where you going?" he inquired as he drew face to face with me.

"Good afternoon," I said. "Might I say that I am marveling at how there are hardly any wrinkles in your uniform on this very hot day. And what a clean car you have. And, oh, yes, I was going to Tucson to visit my very sick aunt who lives near the airport."

"Well, you're in luck. I'm out of my jurisdiction anyway. I'm heading back after dropping off a prisoner. Airport's not that far out of my way. Hop in. Whatcha got in that bag? Donuts?"

"As a matter of fact, I do," I said. "I'd be mighty glad to let you have them, and I'll be content with the Fritos."

"Mister, you got a deal," he said and opened the door for me. "Don't forget your seat belt. Hate to have to give you a ticket for riding without a seat belt. My name's Slick. Slick Rhodes. What's yours?"

Sheriff Rhodes had seen my license yesterday, and although it was clearer than ever that the wattage in his light bulb was on the low side, I chose a new name. "Woodward," I said. "Tom Woodward."

"Well, Mr. Woodward, you're fortunate I came along. This stretch of road is a dangerous place. Why, yesterday I happened on a man — looked a lot like you — and he cold-cocked me. Some kind of new criminal element from Massatwoshits. Then the sonofabitch went down to Sandy Creek and we lost track of him. Got his car, but turns out the guy had stolen a rental. Big man, did I tell you. Yeah, about your size. Lethal though. What a punch. We're probably going to be calling in the Special Crimes Task Force. Assaulting an officer of the law is a felony."

I opened up the bag of Hostess powdered donuts and handed them to him, one by one. After a few, his barely wrinkled shirt was covered with snowy white droppings. And his chin. And the tip of his nose. The man, however, did appreciate his donuts, and I respected him for it.

By the time we got to Tucson, he insisted on taking me straight to my sick aunt's home. I told him I couldn't remember the address but could otherwise direct him. After a tour through a dense industrial district, I spotted a house that could have been my aunt's if I'd had a living aunt. No need to wait, I said, we always go in through the back door.

The airport was but a twenty-minute walk away.

CHAPTER SIX

As it turned out, Mary Ellen was very happy to have me home, having grown tired of her sister's faux interest in our affairs. She'd picked me up after I'd claimed my lost luggage from my first return to Hartford. All's well that ends well, I suppose, but I was going to have to find another wig. That trick had worked out great.

"So are you giving up this private investigator dream once and for all?" she asked when we pulled out of the Bradley complex.

"Not at all. I'm more committed than ever," I answered. "You should have seen me in action. You'd have been proud. I was not only at the top of my class at college, I saved a little boy's life, I punched a guy, and I think I've uncovered an international crime syndicate."

"You've what? Dickie, you listen to me. Enough with the cops and robbers stuff, okay? I told my sister that she could forget about me moving in because I was getting my husband back. And I want my husband back, you got that?"

"Mary Ellen, I am back. But I gotta do what I gotta do. You wouldn't want me hanging around the house, following you to the grocery store, checking up on your meal preparations, eavesdropping on your phone calls would you? Of course not. I haven't had so much fun since I had my television show."

"Some television show. First, you paid for the time from your wedding money. Secondly, nobody watched it. Third, even when you offered to double what you were paying, the station said they'd have you arrested if you showed up again. You call that fun?"

"Yes, it was. It was different. And the thing was, I didn't know what would happen next. I was always on edge. And this is exactly like that. I just want to follow up one lead and see where it goes. Then I'll be in touch with Myron and settle down to a quieter life."

We rode the rest of the way home pretty much in silence except for her occasional harrumph.

I proposed a dinner that night at the new Doubletree Hotel's restaurant in Bristol. Their advertisements boasted they were across the street from ESPN, and I had the urge to begin sniffing out what I could sniff out. Over the years, I'd driven past ESPN a few times, always agog at their huge campus. I was no less impressed this time: it's gigantic.

"Dickie, we should come for a tour of ESPN sometime," the woman sitting across from me in the restaurant said, the woman who happened to be Mary Ellen.

"Dickie, you spit soup on your front," she said. "As I always say, you can dress him up, but you'd better leave him at home." (I told you she said that.) I hadn't begun to formulate a plan to for how to get inside ESPN, and now my dear wife had solved the problem.

Public tours of the ESPN properties are held daily at 10 AM, and we returned the next morning, anxious to make up for lost together-time. Though the tours cover only a portion of the 120-plus acres, it was fun to peer into studios prepared for broadcasting, see their fabulous cafeteria, and note the corridor where their "On-Air Personalities'" offices were located. Mary Ellen was impressed, also. Although her love of sports is limited to the UConn Husky women, she did spot Chris Wilson coming out of the men's room. There was a time when she'd join me watching SportsCenter just to hear him do his famous home run call, "The park can't hold it!" She instinctively put out her hand to shake his and was rewarded by a very wet exchange that left her muttering about the possibilities all the way home.

"You want to do what?" my supposed friend Chief Bob Blaney shouted. I'd just begun to outline my plans in his office later that afternoon when he interrupted me, rudely I thought. "You're not licensed to investigate a gopher sighting, reverend. You can't go nosing around ESPN, making wild accusations based on some two-bit theory you came up with. So help me, you get yourself arrested, you'd better not mention my name."

"Bob," I said. "I'm just going to ask to see Guy O'Neal, tell him what I've learned, and see what he says."

"Have you lost your mind? Not that there's a chance he'd see a nobody like you anyway, but if he did and you said what you said you're going to say, he'd say get the hell lost!" Bob had a way with words.

He was also probably right. But there was a chance he was wrong. And I had nothing better to do, anyway.

***

"Weren't you here yesterday?" asked the guide with a badge saying "Fern – ESP-In Your Face Escort."

"I don't believe so," I said, instantly revealing my impending dementia.

I tried to hang toward the rear of the group of twenty or so. For one reason, I'd spotted too late yesterday an opportunity to grab a muffin from an unattended cart in the cafeteria; for another, there was less of a chance of being noticed entering the hallway to the "personalities'" offices. Sad to say, they caught me snatching a muffin ("Those aren't for the tour, sir"); I wasn't caught entering the suite of offices.

You'd think highly paid prima donna types would have their own wood-paneled offices, several layers of assistants each at their own desks, but they don't. They have gray-walled cubbies with nameplates that one could buy online. On the perimeter of the large room with the cubbies are conference rooms presumably for when two or more want to go talk about the boss or something. Otherwise, it's pretty much like you see on their TV commercials, except I didn't spot any famous athletes walking around in shorts or hockey pads.

After nodding hello to a few people who looked familiar from SportsCenter, I came to Guy O'Neal's cubby. No one was home, so I sat in his chair. In case you're wondering where this bold streak of mine came from, it isn't a new thing. As a pastor, many was the time I had to insinuate myself into a situation where most people wouldn't have strayed. One time there was a man, who shall remain nameless, who had been skipping church for weeks claiming he was ill. So one Sunday I decided to show up at his house early in the afternoon. "George Daniels!" I shouted when he opened the door. "You don't look sick to me." Whereupon he fell to the ground, clutching his heart. At his funeral, I was quick to say that I'd been wrong, he really had been sick. But you get the point; when I feel I'm right, when justice must be served, I'll be as intrepid as the situation calls for.

I was admiring Mr. O'Neal's many certificates and a couple of his Emmys when a very tall man in a security uniform appeared in the doorway. Maybe an out-of-work basketball player. "Who are you?" he rumbled.

"I'm a friend of a friend," I said, standing to meet his gaze, which still left me several inches short. "Just dropped in to say 'hi' to

Guy. Hey, that's pretty good. Hi, Guy. Or Guy, Hi."

"Well Guy's away, not due back until tonight. You'll have to leave. How'd you get in here anyway?"

"Fern told me I had free rein, to enjoy myself," I said hoping to get the tour guide in some kind of trouble for grabbing the muffin out of my hand.

"So you know your way out, then," he said. "Please leave."

I did.

I returned home to Hillsdale and set about researching Guy O'Neal's local address, a task that required no more than two minutes. Between Google and whitepages.com, you can find addresses of virtually every person alive and many who are dead. Whitepages had a G O'Neal, age 45–50, living at 2 Mattes Circle in Avon. I'd heard that Avon was home to a bunch of ESPN celebrities where the average home goes for around five hundred thousand bucks, and million-plus ones are common. It's also convenient to blue collar, industrial Bristol – maybe thirty minutes, depending on traffic.

Mary Ellen had scheduled a night out with our daughter, Lucy, to make plans for a wedding shower they were giving for a friend.

Nevertheless, because I don't like keeping things from her, I told her my plans. "I'll just sit in a car outside his house, and when he returns I'll introduce myself and tell him that Rusty and Jasmine say 'hi.' He's a little short, chubby fellow with a girlish giggle. I'm not worried about violence."

"If you're not home by midnight, Dickie, I'm calling the police," she said. But that was all she said, which I interpreted as permission to proceed apace.

The security guard had said Guy was due back that night, which to me meant any time from six on – on to morning. I really hoped earlier than later. In consideration for my preferences, at nine a Lexus pulled into the O'Neal driveway. As the electric-powered garage door inched upwards, a person emerged from the passenger side and began walking down the sloping pavement towards the mailbox. If I didn't know better, I'd have sworn it was Jasmine.

CHAPTER SEVEN

It *was* Jasmine. Talk about a wrench thrown into the works.

I watched her gather a large bundle of mail to her bosom, climb the steep lawn, and enter through the front door, opened for her by Guy. I was stunned. I knew Jasmine hadn't been on the plane with me because I'd walked the aisle twice to make sure. Of course, she could've beaten me home on another flight or met up with Guy, wherever he was. In the last analysis, of course, who cared how she got there – she got there.

I was buying time with my dithering because I didn't know what else to do. Fortunately, I didn't have to purchase many more dithering minutes as a second car, a Smart car, backed out of the garage with Jasmine at the wheel. I followed.

I wondered if she was headed to the airport, but a left turn onto Route 10 was taking us in the opposite direction. Another right, another left, and Jasmine eventually pulled in to a 7-Eleven in Unionville. I suspect at one time 7-Eleven meant open from 7 to 11. Since a sign in the window now boasted "Open 24 hours for your shopping pleasure – free worms," I deemed a name change in order, not to mention a new sign maker.

I hastily parked in the space next to Jasmine's driver-side door and intercepted her before she could enter the store. "Who are you? What do you want?" she asked, feigning fear.

I had to admit she was pretty good. "Jasmine, cut it out. It's me, Richard, or Dick, if you insist. What are you up to?"

"I have no idea who you are or what you're talking about. I'm dialing 911, and if you try to stop me I'll scream," Jasmine said, pulling her phone from her purse.

For some reason, Jasmine had attached a large fake mole on her cheek. Clever disguise. I picked at it. For some reason, the mole resisted picking. She screamed.

I was grabbed roughly by a man I presumed to be the night manager and a passerby who asked me if I had any loose change.

The non-fake mole had made me question my detecting ability. Otherwise, it was Jasmine. Or her twin.

"Hey," I said, "do you have a sister named Jasmine?"

"It's none of your business," she replied. "What kind of a person would scratch another person's face? You need psychiatric help!"

"The police are on their way," the manager said, "I pulled the alarm before I came out. Mister, if you're wise, you'll hightail it out of here while you can."

The passerby dude seemed not to care for my welfare. "How about a twenty? Just a twenty? Come on, man, I haven't eaten in a month. A ten then. Surely you got a ten, you piece of —"

And to think I could once charm the socks off people.

The Jasminish woman then surprised me. "I think I know who you are. Come on, let's take a ride."

I'd never ridden in a two-seat Smart car before, and it would be fine with me if I never did again. It's very hard to talk with your knees in your face, but I did my best.

"My name is Chamomile," Jasmine's twin with the mole said as we sped out of the 7-Eleven, passing a police car with lights and siren on its way in. "Our parents liked tea. I understand my mother wanted to name me

Constant Comment, after her favorite. But my dad put his foot down. So I count myself lucky. Jasmine told me about you, said she was so sorry to get you involved in the mess she's in. Actually, the mess we're both in. I need to tell you about it so you'll understand why you have to leave us alone. And then I must ask you to leave us alone. Nothing good can come from you pursuing this any further."

An hour later and blown out of my mind with the details of Jasmine and Chamomile's situation, I was returned to the 7-Eleven. The night manager waved from inside, suggesting I had nothing to fear from the law. The other gentleman was nowhere to be found, but I suspected the upside-down strawberry Slurpee on the hood of my car was his calling card. The sight made me hungry nonetheless. Believe me: 7-Eleven's hot dogs on the little rolling tubes are every bit as good as the Circle K's in Arizona. Don't let anyone tell you differently.

I told Chamomile I'd cease and desist, but for the next several days I couldn't stop thinking about the twins. I thought about sharing what I'd learned with Bob the police chief, but I knew his motto was "If it didn't happen in Hillsdale, I don't give a crap." So I told Mary Ellen.

"Passports," I said. "Fake passports. Rusty's an expert at making passports, creating them from scratch. Camouflage passports are their technical name. It's become a major international problem. One of Rusty's contacts somehow linked him up with Guy O'Neal. Now O'Neal takes orders from people with money who can't get their own for one reason or another and delivers them in person when he goes to do his ESPN taping. His whole criteria for which star to highlight has to do with the area of the world he has the most orders from. Chamomile said he transports them, ten or so at a time, sewn into his clothes."

"Doesn't he ever get searched?" Mary Ellen asked.

"No, that's the other clever thing about this. First, he's a well-known celebrity and always flies out of Bradley where every person up there is on a first-name basis with him. And secondly, he's a short, pudgy guy with a bunch of bulges and rolls of his own. I mean, the whole scheme is almost divinely inspired, if I say so myself. And you know how much he charges for each? Five thousand dollars! O'Neal gives Rusty $500 for each and keeps the rest. He's making a freaking fortune!"

"You said Chamomile referred to it as a mess. What's her problem? She want more of a cut?"

"Chamomile and Jasmine are undocumented. Rusty has a daughter with Jasmine, though Jasmine now despises Rusty. They both do what he wants because he says he'll report them if they don't, and keep Jasmine from taking the kid back to Mexico."

"But I don't understand," Mary Ellen said. "If everyone's making so much money, why did they target you and that other man? You don't even *look* rich."

"I asked Chamomile the same question. She said Rusty almost always gets some kind of information from a man's billfold that helps him make realistic IDs. Often enough, they come up with an official passport, and somehow that makes his job even easier. Since Jasmine flies the passports to Guy every month, she encounters plenty of potential stooges on her return flights. Plus, Rusty appreciates scoring untraceable cash to support his cocaine habit. The man's an entrepreneurial whiz, what can I say?"

Mary Ellen suggested I notify the FBI or CIA or one of the agencies involved in international crime. But, come on now, who would they believe – me or a famous ESPN guy? I'd be locked up for impersonating a normal person. I had another idea.

CHAPTER EIGHT

In our drive around the Hartford suburbs, Chamomile told me that Rusty and Guy had assigned her to be Guy's gofer. In return, she got a nice little apartment, the tiny car, and a decent salary. She'd also divulged that they were going to Lichtenstein next Monday. Seems there was a high jumper in that small country bordered by Switzerland and Austria destined to bring home the first summer Olympics medal. It was also a certainty that there would be around ten bad-dude Liechtensteiners waiting for their $5,000 passports.

I could hardly wait until Monday, and managed to locate a good wig in the Meriden Shopping Center. This one was blond and much less curly, a mannish-enough looking wig. I wanted to show it to Mary Ellen for her approval, but that would have to wait. In fact, I'd told Mary Ellen a bit of a white lie – okay a whopper, but it was for a good cause, okay? – saying I'd come to a dead end; I was throwing in the towel. Then, early Monday morning, I left a note saying I was going to Starbucks for coffee and pastries and to read the *Times*. If my plan worked, I figured I'd be back before Morning Joe was over.

The best way by far to get from Hartford's Bradley International Airport to Lichtenstein is via Air Canada to Toronto and through to Zurich. From there you can drive or take a train the rest of the way. Doing all the flying on one airline also means no heavy-duty security in Toronto or another airport. Researching what O'Neal would surely do wasn't hard: To make a Monday morning flight to the above destinations limited the options to but one Air Canada departure at 8 AM.

I was cutting it close, but didn't want to draw too much attention to my blond condition. I entered the terminal around 6 AM and put a newspaper in front of my face, sneaking a glance at the Air Canada counter from time to time. At 6:20, Guy and Chamomile walked in, each pulling a carry-on. He also had a large piece of luggage. They checked the large suitcase and headed for the TSA screening ritual.

Now don't forget that I've enjoyed no little celebrity in my 30 or so years of ministry. I know what it's like for people to do double takes, smile, and greet me somewhat deferentially, respectable man of God as I was deemed to be. So, I wasn't unprepared to witness the treatment O'Neal got from fellow passengers and airline employees. But whereas after seeing me people often put their head down and go in another direction, the famous Guy O'Neal was attracting followers like flies on an elephant. This would make my job harder – harder, but not impossible.

I shoved my way through hangers-on while calling out his name, as if I were an old friend from the past. "Guy! Oh, Guy!" The flies parted willingly, suspecting I might be someone else they knew from the tube. When Guy turned around to see who the excited person was, I grabbed at his sport coat, ripped it off his back, and tore his shirt right to left exposing the flabbiest, hairiest multiple mounds of skin fighting with each other for sunshine imaginable. And that was all. He was half-naked, uglier than ugly, but not a passport in sight. His shirt, obviously, was innocent. His coat, however, was another matter. Hands slipped on and off me, attempting to slow my progress, but I managed to fondle every inch of his expensive jacket. Bottom line: I could have testified in a court of law that there was nothing there but wool cloth, and most of it in one degree or another of tatters.

In the flurry of activity, my handsome blond wig had come loose and was being kicked from one person to another as if it were alive and posed a deadly threat. Meanwhile, Chamomile looked on as if my bare-headedness might somehow indict her. I'd managed to avoid capture for more seconds than Las Vegas oddsmakers would have bet, but it wasn't long before my hands were yanked behind me and securely held in place by metal cuffs squeezed far tighter than they needed to be. I'm a lover, remember, not a fighter, though a tad late to boast about such at that point. And, it's true: they really do read you your rights and ask if you understand them before throwing you in the back of a cop car.

They said I could make one phone call. I was being held in what appeared to be a jail on the Bradley Airport grounds. Before that day, I couldn't have told you which law enforcement agency had oversight at the airport. However, since "Connecticut State Police" was written on everything, it must have been them. The only attorney Mary Ellen and I had ever used majored in real estate and minored in wills.

Since there wasn't anything in this for him, I didn't want to waste my dime there. I also pondered calling Bob, the Hillsdale chief, but he'd already told me not to bother if I got in trouble. So, another dime saved. It now being late morning, my stomach was growling for lunch so naturally I thought of Domino's. Didn't know, though, if they delivered to convicts. That left Mary Ellen.

"Hi, honey, what's up?" I announced cheerily.

"Where are you? How many donuts have you had, anyway?"

"Would you believe none? But that's not why I'm calling. Can you get in touch with your friend who works for that lawyer who's always in the news and see if he'd take my case? I sorta got arrested at Bradley."

"Dickie Burgess, you'd better be playing a joke on me!"

"The passports must have been in his pants," I said.

"What passports? In whose pants?"

"Guy O'Neal must carry the passports in his pants, not his shirt. I guessed wrong. Oh, and sweetie, you'd better call Matt and Lucy and tell them their dad's likely going to be the lead story on both the national news and

SportsCenter. I think they'd appreciate knowing beforehand."

After talking with Atticus Klinkenborg of Klinkenborg, Klinkenborg and Klinkenborg, LLC, I took advantage of prisoner privileges that amounted to a bench in a large room with a television from the 90s. For company, I had four guys who each said they'd been framed. Since I couldn't very well claim the same defense, they were not impressed with me. ESPN was on channel 36, and all agreed to watch it.

"ESPN's own Guy O'Neal was in the news today as a lunatic lunged at him, tearing off his coat and shirt. Rev. Richard Burgess, former pastor of the Hillsdale Community Church, was arrested at Bradley International Airport and charged with assault and battery and use of a deadly weapon, identified as a small, blond animal. Guy was unhurt, and following a brief statement to police, was able to board his flight, which will take him eventually to Liechtenstein where he will interview Pietr Boreskind, a high jumper and Olympic hopeful, for his popular ESPN program *Very Important Nobodies*."

A clip was played of me being turkey-walked to the cruiser, and another of me being escorted into the jail. My friends in crime in the group room were now very impressed with me. "You really tried to off that TV dude? Man, you be bad!"

"Yeah, I'm bad, I'm bad," I said, hoping to discourage any late night attack on me. I was now known as a violent nutcase, a reputation I needed to use to my benefit.

Matt flew up from DC where he works for one of the 17 alphabet-named government agencies whose main business is spying. Whatever he does is obviously top secret. But, since he's a computer whiz, I'd guess he has a desk job. In any case, he can't say and I don't ask. He brought Mary Ellen and his sister, Lucy, with him the next morning.

"Dad, I gotta say this is not what I learned in confirmation class." Matt was the blunter of our children. Lucy, on the other hand, brought flowers from the shop where she worked and a book on Zen. "You need to learn how to live in the moment, Dad. Just flow. Don't think about the past or the future. Just be." That's our Lucy: idealistic to the point of absurdity but always lovable.

I tried to remain cheerful over the next several days, but with nothing to look forward to other than meals and a daily visit from

Attorney Klinkenborg, I'd gotten depressed. The book on Zen helped as long as I didn't think about anything. But I had so much to think about that I wondered if the book's author had ever lived in the real world of death and taxes and…steel bars.

Mary Ellen visited a couple of times with greetings from the kids, who'd each gone back to their own busy lives. She said the *Register* and local stations had been hounding her for interviews, but she'd referred everyone to our expensive attorney. She also said several of my former flock had called, some with sympathy, and more than a few angry that I would do anything to besmirch the fine name of their church. Honestly, I couldn't agree more. I'd done my best to do some good but had bungled everything, plus made a fool of myself, plus brought discredit to innumerable churchly people. Then there was the reality I might live the rest of my days in jail. And, not least, Jasmine and Chamomile were no better off for all my folly.

I awoke on Friday to my cell door squeaking open. This was more than breakfast, I said to my waking self, which I'd come to find on a shelf this side of an opening in the bars.

"Burgess, we've got orders to transport you to the Hartford pen," a trooper said, his hat cocked so low I couldn't imagine he'd ever seen the sun. "Don't know why, but come with me."

Honestly, this development scared me. My new BFFs and I were getting along nicely, and I wasn't excited about making new acquaintances among the criminal element.

I was re-cuffed and led to curbside. Rain was in the air, which meant in July the humidity was so thick it had its own humidity. A van with the state police logo pulled up, and my handler popped open the back end, boosted me up, and shoved me toward a bench. Sitting with one's hands literally tied behind oneself is not comfortable for very long, especially if you're over 50. In 30 seconds, I was close to writhing in agony.

"How you doin' back there, Kemosabe?"

CHAPTER NINE

"Eagle! For crying out loud! What are you doing here? How'd you know where to find me? How'd you get here?"

"You ask strange questions for a man whose bacon has just been saved," Eagle replied. "But I'll answer them in order: one, I'm driving you to your freedom; two, Arizona may not be Connecticut, but we do get ESPN, and I saw you doing the perp walk. Thought I told you to lose your preppie clothes; three, I drove my car. Speaking of my car, you up to a little walk?"

"Walk? What do you mean?"

"I couldn't very well leave the Vette in the space next to where I found this police van, now could I? We got to ditch the van and then hike to my car. Okay with you?"

"Oh, Lord! I'm going to be in such big trouble! What are you planning to do?"

"This Guy O'Neal is a bad man, and Mary Ellen told me about Rusty. He's bad, too. We've got to finish what you started and expose him. Though not, may I suggest, by ripping off his clothes."

"Mary Ellen knows what you're doing?" I stammered.

"She only knows I called to check up on you. She seems the anxious type. Not given to cloak-and-dagger stuff. How'd you ever think you could be a detective with such a wonderful woman worrying about you all the time?"

That was, to say the least, a question for which I didn't have an answer. I had two choices. One was to jump out of the van and tell the first officer I saw that I'd been kidnapped. That would be entirely believable, and I could go safely back to my cell and wait for my eternal punishment. Or, with Eagle's help, I could try one more time to shake down Mr. O'Neal before the law caught up to us. I chose the latter.

Luckily, our walk from the cul-de-sac in a condo complex where we left the police van to where Eagle's black Corvette awaited us was more a stroll than a hike. It also led us past a McDonald's, and that was fine with me. Too many days without fast food aren't good for a body. My prison garb consisted of a roadside orange jumpsuit. No lettering or numbers, thank goodness. Still, I drew lots of quizzical glances and a few downright hostile stares – we were on the edge of a posh suburb, you see, and I was undoubtedly violating some code of clothing decency.

After finishing my second Quarter Pounder (hold the cheese, I don't need the calories), I tried out an idea on Eagle. "Say one of us went to O'Neal's house, and say one of us claimed to be an angry relative of an unhappy passport customer demanding our five K back, and say we picked up the right kind of electronic equipment so that the conversation could be taped and then say we played a confession by any other name before the world. What do you think would happen?"

"Well, first of all," Eagle began, "I'd bet they'd take his show off the air, which would be too bad because it's one of my favorites."

"That's all you got to say? Don't you think it's pure genius?"

"How long have we known each other?" Eagle asked.

"I don't know. Ten days, two weeks, from whenever I saved your boy."

"You mean from whenever I saved your life in the storage bin."

"Okay, that. Right. From then."
"My point," Eagle said slowly as if normal

paced speech would have confused me, "my point is that whatever you are, *genius* could never be used to describe you."

"Point taken. But besides losing your favorite show, are you game to try?"

"Does sound like fun. Don't have a better idea. Too bad he wouldn't want to fight me. I like to fight but most folks are too scared to try. Haven't had a fight in ages. So where do we get the stuff we'd need?"

I called Matt using Eagle's car's Bluetooth connection. He told me what we'd need and where we could purchase said devices. I said "we," but I should've said "Eagle," because a BOLO had now been put out for me and my orange formal wear. An escaped convict is big news in Connecticut, and even the smooth jazz station Eagle was listening to broke in to alert the citizenry.

The Ye Olde Colony Spy Shop had recently opened on Pearl Street in Hartford, a branch of the same in Manhattan. From what I've read, little cameras and recording devices are "must-have" items these days. Go figure. Eagle wasn't gone long, returning as the proud owner of a new pen to join the others in his pocket protector. This one, though, had set him back a thousand bucks and couldn't scribble a doodle. But it did have a camera, microphone, and high-capacity chip for recording. Oh, and did I mention it also could connect to the Internet? Even came loaded with an app to open a YouTube account. Imagine that.

I figured O'Neal would be home at 11 on a work night, probably watching SportsCenter. And he was. Thanks to a well-placed streetlight in O'Neal's Avon neighborhood, I could watch as Eagle made his way to the front porch and rang the bell.

O'Neal came to the door, inched it open warily, then apparently confirming that the very big man with a menacing face was indeed the same as the one he'd seen through the peephole, attempted to slam it shut. Eagle's size 20-or-so foot prevented that from happening. Life, as Guy O'Neal had known it, would soon be over.

***

"Who are you? I'm going to call the police!" O'Neal said, staring at Eagle's humongous shoe while revealing a top-view of the worst comb-over television has ever seen.

"Mr. O'Neal, let us just say I'm a very dissatisfied customer. The passport you made for my brother is junk. We want our $5,000 back."

"I don't know what you're talking about," O'Neal tried, hitching up what appeared to be a size Triple-X pair of cargo shorts. "You must have me confused with someone else. I'm a sports broadcaster, not the passport agency. Now please leave or I'll call the police."

"Funny you say you don't know what I'm talking about. I'll bet you do know Rusty in Tucson, though, don't you?"

"Rusty? I don't know anyone named Rusty. Now get off my porch!"

"Sure you know Rusty. Makes passports. You fit them in your pants. You travel to far-off places and sell them for $5,000. *That* Rusty."

"Did that little punk put you up to this? Is this a shakedown? He trying to make a little extra? You tell him to go to hell. He's not going to receive another dime from me. I'm working on another supplier, anyway. I don't need him anymore. Now, get out of here. I've got my finger on an alarm that will have the police here in two minutes. I'm warning you – get lost!"

Eagle wasn't given to smiling much. Which is why as he folded himself into the car I knew his ear-to-ear grin meant victory was at hand. No one knows how or why videos go viral on YouTube. They just do. And this one did, too.

CHAPTER TEN

Late the next afternoon, I went to Chief Blaney's Hillsdale office. The usual box of Dunkin' Donuts graced the corner of his desk. There was only one apple fritter remaining amidst the powdered sugar and crumbs. Bob reached for it and I slapped his hand. He grudgingly let me take it.

"I've been in touch with the State Police," he said, "and they have a bunch of paperwork and court stuff that you'll need to work out, but in any event, the charges are being dropped. There's also some issue about filming someone without their permission, but they don't think O'Neal has the stomach to pursue such a minor complaint. So, basically, you're good to go. Oh, almost forgot. They'd like their jumpsuit back. Budget cuts, you know."

I got in touch with Eagle a couple of days later, after he'd driven straight through to Sandy Creek. I was concerned for what Rusty might do to Jasmine and Chamomile in light of my intervention. One little word from him could mean big trouble for them.

I shouldn't have worried, however. Eagle said Rusty had already been arrested and released on bail, and that he'd found him at his filling station. "He won't be giving anybody trouble," Eagle said. "He knows his future interests will best be served by leaving the women out of it. Trust me."

"Eagle, I don't condone violence. Okay?"

"No problem. But Rusty doesn't know that. Told him I'd sic half the prison population on him if he even hinted at knowing Jasmine or Chamomile. He's scared out of his mind."

"Do you know where Jasmine is?" I asked.

"No, Rusty said as soon as they heard about the YouTube video she grabbed their daughter and beat it. My two cents' worth? I don't think he would've turned them in. The threat worked. That's all he cared about."

"All's well that ends well," I said. "We did some good, you and I. Wish we lived closer. I might need some help if this PI thing gets off the ground."

"Something tells me picking up after you would be a full-time job. I mean, you're a piece of work, you know that, Richard?"

"I'm sure Mary Ellen would agree. In any case, thanks Eagle. Give Frankie my regards."

"Will do. He said you have a right cross better than mine. You're the man in his book."

"I'll remember that," I said. "The best thing anyone's said about me in years."

"He also said he wanted a pair of white sneakers like you."

"Really? I'll send him a pair of New Balance cross trainers this very afternoon."

"No, Richard. You do that, and I'll come for you. And it won't be pretty."

The End

The Lavender Lexus

Straight out of a Spenser novel, a beautiful, leggy blonde walked into my private detective office, looked me in the eye, and sat down. When I asked how I could help her, she opened her mouth but said not a word.

My dream had finally come true. Following thirty years as pastor of the Hillsdale Community Church, I was now Richard Burgess, Private Investigator. At least that's what the printing on my frosted-glass door says. Technically, I'm on probation in this business, but the licensed PI, Myron Feller, who is to supervise my caseload, has given me carte blanche: "Just don't get arrested" were his parting words before leaving me to admire my new digs. I might otherwise have been grateful for his confidence, but the truth was, thanks to my wife Mary Ellen's inheritance, I'd set Myron and I up in a handsome suite in a tiny strip mall in Hillsdale, Connecticut. Still, I might have been at least somewhat in his debt but for the other reality: Myron is in the top ten of the world's laziest people. He was giving me nothing. After two years of an unblemished record as his "assistant," I would qualify for my own Connecticut license. Were it up to Myron, he'd sign it today. He didn't care. In fact, I couldn't identify one thing Myron did care about except not working.

So, if there is gratitude due, it's to the Hillsdale Police Chief, Bob Blaney, a longtime friend with whom I'd worked as a volunteer police chaplain when I was a minister. Bob helped me negotiate some paperwork and found Myron, an ex-cop, for me to shadow. What I really like about Bob is that if you Google his name plus Dunkin' Donuts, you get his picture. Bob always has a box on his desk. And he saves the glazed sticks for me.

So, this blonde walks in through my open door, sits and looks me in the eye. And begins panting. A beautiful golden retriever. It's true, I did ask her what I might do for her, but I honestly didn't expect an answer – it was an opening line I'd learned in my weeklong course in Tucson at the So You Want To Be A Private Investigator College. Being new in this line of work, I didn't want to color too far outside the lines with what might be my first customer.

She didn't remain quiet for long – a polite, ladylike bark came forth. She then approached my desk, put her front paws up next to my picture of Mary Ellen, snatched a glazed stick from the box of Dunkin' Donuts that Chief Bob had given as an office-warming present, and tossed it back. I'll tell you, this didn't seem like the beginning of a beautiful friendship. I grabbed the remaining one and joined her in savoring the incomparable delicacy. She finished first – I don't think she chews her food as thoroughly as doctors advise. After an ungirlish belch, she barked much louder than before and made a start for the door, turning her head to see if I was following. I was.

There were perhaps a dozen cars in the parking lot. Midafternoon was a little early for the Chinese restaurant to have customers, meaning the cars' occupants must be busy in either the urgent care clinic, paint store, nail salon, or cleaners. One car stood out, in part because it was parked farthest from the mall, half on the grass and about five feet from the state highway that gives the mall its name, Route 50 Shoppes. It also stood out because it was lavender in color – a lavender Lexus SUV. My new best friend made a beeline for it.

With a back window rolled all the way down, I surmised the dog must have grown tired of her perch and not being able to have her cheeks filled by rushing wind. I wondered if the driver had chosen to park in such a remote location to avoid scratches; I'd imagine a lavender Lexus SUV might invite a few door bangs for karma's sake.

I approached the driver's side from the front, my view hindered by deeply tinted glass. I didn't expect to find someone inside but there was. I couldn't make out male or female – not that it mattered, of course. Still, who would let their dog jump out a window? When a knock on the glass and a boisterous "hello" returned no invitation, I opened the door to find an attractive fortyish woman with her head down and her hands resting primly in her lap. "Ma'am," I said. "Is this dog yours?" For the second time in the last ten minutes, a female had refused to answer my question. This time, however, it was because the female was dead.

It hadn't been obvious at first. Her eyes were open, and she seemed merely lost in thought. In fact, it wasn't until I tapped her shoulder to get her attention that she fell out of the car at my feet.

Chief Blaney came himself after I called 911. Murders are rare in Hillsdale, as in once-every-hundred-years rare. He rummaged around in his trunk for yellow crime scene tape, finally finding a roll under a coat on the rear floorboard. Even without an odd murder or two, there aren't many crimes of any kind in Hillsdale where the weekly paper gives headlines to someone ticketed for driving 50 in a 35 mph zone.

"Now don't disturb nothin' 'cause what we have here is a crime scene," he said before letting two paramedics under the tape.

"Chief, we have to try to resuscitate her if we want to get paid. How're we supposed to do that if we don't disturb her at least a little bit?"

"Well, I don't know – that's your problem. By the way, who the hell am I supposed to call when something like this happens? Richard, you have any idea?"

I didn't.

"Guess I'll phone the state troopers," Bob said. "They're used to stuff like this and have them fancy CSI kits and whatnot." He warily advanced closer to the body as if not sure whether it might jump up and bite him. "You sure she's not sleeping? I don't see any blood."

"Chief, she's deader than a doornail," one of the paramedics said, before shoving his stethoscope into his back pocket. "Won't need lights and siren for this."

I'd been careful not to go inside the cordoned-off area out of respect for Bob's crime scene, but I attracted no attention when I did. And the reason I did had to do with a foil cupcake liner I'd spied sticking out from under the woman's arm on the pavement where she'd fallen. It was a lavender paisley design that matched the car's color. I should probably have given the piece of pretty trash to Bob, but I knew he'd probably just throw it back on the ground. So I stuffed it into my pocket. Lavender isn't all that common a color; two lavender items near a dead person was certainly worth some pondering.

"I'd say we're nearly done here," Bob said. "State Police will want to follow up with the hospital. Unless I'm supposed to. I'm getting a headache just thinking about all the details. Wait! Where's her purse? She's gotta have a purse. How're we supposed to know who she is?"

A thorough search turned up no purse, wallet, or anything personal. The registration in the glove compartment disclosed that the car was registered to a bunch of initials, Inc., and a White Plains, New York address.

"Richard, care to join me at the Eat and Whiz for a coffee?" Bob asked. "Then I've got to start the paperwork."

The Eat and Whiz was Hillsdale's only other restaurant besides the Chinese in the shopping center. If you wanted to eat something better than what your least favorite aunt could cook, you went into New Haven or one of the nicer suburbs. The Eat and Whiz came by its name in an unusual way. It had been born as Two Guys Restaurant and lived happily for decades. But when the national Two Guys chain took them to court to force them to change their name, the locals didn't have enough money to contest the suit. So, they decided to protest with a name no one could forget. And, believe me, no one forgets the name of the Eat and Whiz. They were interviewed once by the *New Haven Register* and explained they chose the name because that's what most of the people did when they patronized the place. I think they were exaggerating.

I told the chief I had other things to do. And the main other thing I had to do was to take care of the golden retriever until the police could determine who the dead woman's family was.

***

"You're bringing home what? A dog? Dickie, I don't want to have to take care of a dog." Mary Ellen wasn't enthused to receive my phone call.

"But, it'll only be for a day or two until we can locate the woman's next of kin," I tried.

"Well, okay, but you have to keep her with you the whole time. If you're going to be out playing private eye, I don't want to be saddled with taking her for walks to do her business."

"Fair enough," I said, reaching to pat my blonde friend, whose big smile suggested she knew her next meal was now guaranteed.

"And get yourself something to eat, Dickie. I forgot my book club is meeting at the Italian Garden in New Haven for dinner. I'll be home around 8 unless Mavis has too much wine and won't stop talking."

She'd responded with five of my favorite words: "Get yourself something to eat." Mary Ellen was a wonderful woman but a mediocre cook at best, and I certainly had no culinary skills. Any excuse for fast food was always heaven sent.

The dog seemed as happy as I at the sight of the McDonald's sign. Something told me she'd done this before, and insisted on sitting in the jump seat drooling as we aimed for the drive-thru. Quarter Pounder, medium fries, Diet Coke. And a Happy Meal for my friend.

We ate in silence in a parking space, save for some lip smacking by the party to my right. Because she was done in less than ten seconds, she eyed my food and me, her head bobbing with each bite. Even though I gave her every other fry in my container, her cold stare suggested if we weren't such good friends she might jump down my throat for the rest. I knew I had to get her home and empty the newly purchased dog food bags to keep her from thoughts of patricide.

After depositing our paper products in the trash can like good citizens, I called Chief Blaney. "Turn up an identity for Jane Doe yet?"

"No, the state guys from Farmington are going to go get her from Yale New Haven Hospital. They'll run her fingerprints, do an autopsy, etc., etc. Very odd case. Never had anything like this before. Saw something similar on TV once. But it was a man. Just died. No one could figure out what happened."

I bit. "So what happened?"

"That's the deal. He just died."

"Bob, I can't believe they'd make a television show about a guy who dies for no particular reason."

"Well, maybe I'm confusing it with something else, but I'll tell you, I remember it kept me on the edge of my seat."

***

My new best friend and I were watching the Yankees beat up on the Mariners when Mary Ellen entered from the garage. Blondie leaped off the sofa and embraced Mary Ellen fully and frontally.

"Will you get this hairy monster off me?" she cried.

I tried calling the dog every likely name I could think of, but she was clearly attracted to Mary Ellen or at least the remains of garlic and wine – or maybe it was the clam sauce with the linguini. In any event, Mary Ellen wasn't having a good time.

Not until my wife escaped into our bedroom and slammed the door did the dog give up.

"How long do we have to keep her?" she yelled from her inner sanctum.

"I'm not sure. Will know tomorrow," I said to the door.

"Well, keep her away from me, will you?"

I found a large bowl in the cupboard, filled it with water, and then took the foster dog out for her evening constitutional. "Here, Blondie." "Here, Lassie." "Here, Goldie." "Here, Lady." "Here, Sneakers." The dog seemed amused by the names, but didn't alter her sniffing and piddling act one little bit. No way could I guess her name, of course, but I'd gambled on a few obvious ones. Likely someone driving a lavender Lexus would have chosen a preppie kind of name like Taylor or Swift or Oprah.

I remembered a hilarious Steven Wright routine where the deadpan comedian described a dog he named Stay. Said the dog went insane. I chuckled just recalling it.

"Here, Stay."

A rhododendron prevented me from hitting the ground hard, the dog on top of me, slobber running down my face, into my ears and onto the ground. "Stay" it would be.

***

My cell rang at 7 the next morning. It was Bob. "Thought you'd like to know Jane Doe is no longer Jane Doe."

"Who is she?"

"Who?"

"Jane Doe. What's her real name?" Bob must be the densest man on earth.

"Jane."

"Bob, can we start over? What is the name of the woman who was found dead in a lavender Lexus in the Route 50 Shoppes?"

"Jane."

"Does she have a last name or is she so famous she only needs one?"

"Jane Featherington. She lives or lived on West Farrel Road in Mortonville, according to her sister who had phoned in a missing person's report. Poor thing. Going up to Farmington to identify the body, but sounds like her, lavender Lexus and all. Said her sister – that's Jane – lived alone. Coroner should be finishing up any time. Of course, I shouldn't be telling you all this, but it'll be in the papers anyway."

"Will you call me when the coroner's results are in?" I asked.

"Why? You're not planning on following up on this in any way, are you? State police took charge – don't think you want to get in their way. And, besides, who'd pay you? The dog?"

"Just curious," I lied. "Call me."

With the Petco in Cheshire opening at 9, I told Mary Ellen I'd be back in time to take care of Stay's bodily needs, indoors or outdoors. In search of a doggie bed and some proper dog food, I reckoned that if Stay had a new home tonight, I'd return the bed at least. Thing was, I wasn't sure which way to hope. Except for Mary Ellen's opinion, mine was tending toward a full adoption of Stay.

***

I'd neglected to ask for the sister's name and number from Bob, so I called him en route. "I was going to call you," he said. "Coroner says natural causes."

"What? That's absurd!" I said. "She couldn't be more than 45. You telling me she calmly drove into a mall parking lot and took her last breath?"

"Well, possibly she was on her way to the urgent care place. Who knows? Coroner says it happens. Heart just stops without evidence of disease. Rare, but it occurs more often to women than men. Everything else tested out normal, coroner said."

Many thoughts were running through my head, but I decided not to share any of them with Bob beyond asking for the sister's name and number so I could deliver Stay to her.

After stowing a Petco Doggie Donut bed in brown and a bag of BLUE Buffalo Wilderness dog food into the back of my Outback, I punched the numbers for Jane's sister.

"Ms. Offutt? This is Rev. Burgess, I mean Richard Burgess, I'm so sorry for your loss. I'm the guy who found your sister, Jane. I have her dog."

"You mean Stay?" she said. "I still can't believe my sister's dead. We were together last week. They said they couldn't find a reason for her death, but that makes no sense. She was the healthiest person I know, worked out nearly every day."

"It does seem very odd, but I guess it's more common than we think. I know this is probably the wrong time to bring it up, but I hope you have room for Stay."

"I love Stay, but my husband says no dogs. We've been round and round about it. When

Jane would visit, she'd have to leave Stay in the car…" The remembrance was bringing home her loss more intensely as I heard her sniffling back tears.

"Again, I'm so sorry for this sadness," I said, "but are there other family members who might want Stay?"

"No, there's just the two of us, except for some cousins somewhere. If she had a will, I'm sure she left everything to me."

"So you have no objection to me trying to find a home for Stay with someone else?" I asked.

"No, not at all. You'd be doing me a favor, actually."

Making grief calls in my former life was always the toughest part of my job. Talking Mary Ellen into keeping Stay would be even harder, because that was what my little mind had decided while talking with Jane's sister. Stay had suffered enough trauma – she deserved better. Besides, for the first time in my life, I finally had a friend who shared my taste in food.

With determined steps, I marched into the spare bedroom in which Mary Ellen likes to camp out. My mouth was open to speak impassioned words like how I was 50 percent of this family, and how I'd sacrificed this or that (wasn't sure what I'd come up with), and then saying something like, "It's well known that people with pets live longer," hoping she wouldn't bring up Jane.

I shut my mouth in a hurry. Mary Ellen was napping on the chaise lounge she keeps for her back trouble, and Stay was curled up at the bottom, her head resting softly on Mary Ellen's foot.

She stirred. "Dickie, if that woman's sister doesn't want Stay, do you think we can keep her? She's not so bad. And she really seems to like me."

"Look," I said. "I'm 50 percent of this family. So, okay."

Mary Ellen agreed to call her best friend, Angela, for a vet recommendation and, whistling as she trundled, left the room to scavenge in the basement for some material with which to fashion a kerchief for the newest member of the Burgess clan. "So everyone will know she's a girl," she declared.

Now we had a dog. And I had a dilemma: forget Jane and go sit in my new office and see who walked in; or break into her house with my lock-picking kit from school and search for clues. I had nothing to go on, of course, just a strong intuition that something wasn't right. If this had been the first time I'd felt this way, I'd have dismissed it. But it wasn't. Many was the time in my ministry that one of these hunches turned out to be important. Like when I was counseling a couple who said they had trouble communicating. I'd met with them three or four times and we were getting nowhere. Then, suddenly, while the man was talking, I had this same feeling, this same intuition, hunch. So I blurted out, "You're having an affair with her sister, aren't you?" Turns out he wasn't, but his wife was doing the UPS guy. So I was close.

Same thing with Jane. I knew I may not have it exactly right, but my hunch was saying something smelled funny here, and it had nothing to do with Stay who was now dragging herself across the carpet.

Next day, following a morning visit to the vet who outlined a preventative care plan for Stay, I spent much of the afternoon Googling Jane Featherington, her sister, plus a bunch of other Featheringtons, trying to learn what I could. My conclusion: Jane Featherington lived as mysteriously as she died. I did get a hit on a "J Featherington" who was a Kerry May cosmetics distributor. But the number wasn't local.

After supper and telling Mary Ellen that we were off for some exercise, we went outside and Stay bounded into the back seat of my Subaru Outback and all but pushed the button to lower the glass in her demonstration of what she wanted. Jane Featherington had lived on a well-traveled street in Mortonville. Her modest beige cape was attractive, set back from the road with a detached garage. Dense woods began a hundred or so feet from the back storm door, whose old-fashioned Yale lock proved no obstacle to my newly acquired talent.

Before I could turn on my little penlight, Stay dashed off as on a mission, no doubt in quest of her Jane. My heart tugged a bit when she returned, although she seemed no worse for the fruitless quest. The house was as simple inside as out. It didn't take a private eye, however, to figure out that the Kerry May cosmetics person I'd turned up online was indeed Stay's former owner. Bottles and jars of one thing or another were everywhere. Kerry Clean for floors; Kerry Eyes for eye shadow; Kerry Smell for perfume. Kerry May seemed to have a product for every need.

I didn't have a clue as to what clue I was searching for. Something obvious would have been nice. I looked at Stay, who had found a chew toy on the sofa and was now comfortably biting the bejesus out of it, as content as I was feeling befuddled. "So, girl, what do you think?"

"Well, Richard, I'd say we have a conundrum. Personally, I think a cat did it."

Amusing myself didn't seem to help. Obviously, it was as the coroner said: poor Jane just died.

"Come on, girl, let's get out of here," I said. But instead of following me, Stay sidetracked into the open kitchen and sniffed at a purse on a lower shelf. I don't make a habit of leaving home without my wallet, but I have done it on occasion, and so, too, must have Jane. Inside were typical purse items and a calendar, the kind you can get at Hallmark, though I can't imagine there's much of a run on them given that most people now use a calendar on their phone. Jane's phone was an old-fashioned flip with nothing interesting on the welcome screen. The paper calendar, though, was another matter: Jane was a busy woman, if all the dates and times with *KM* penned in meant anything.

Inspired by my finding, I decided to wade through the garbage container in the kitchen that had revealed itself while my little light was searching through the purse. Yucky paper towels, a soup can, milk carton – she wasn't a recycler – and the prize: several lavender cupcake foils and a few chocolate crumbs.

***

That night I slept fitfully. I dreamed Stay had turned lavender and preferred bagels to donuts. It was a long, tortuous night. I wanted to sing the "Hallelujah" chorus when I awoke.

With coffee cup in hand, I settled into my ergonomic office chair and opened my Mac. Stay felt she could trust me to be alone and left to try to convince Mary Ellen that she hadn't been fed. I knew of Kerry May because of a skin lotion that was discovered to drive mosquitoes into the next state. Checking their website and reading what Bloomberg had to say revealed a Fortune 100 company of international reach. Cosmetics, household cleaning products, over-the-counter vitamins and potions of all sorts – Kerry May was a gigantic conglomerate. "Our products are not sold in stores so we can pass the savings on to you," they boasted. There was an 888 number. I called it.

"Hello, I'm interested in buying some perfume for my wife. How do I get it?" I began.

"I'd be glad to help you. Where do you live, sir?"

"In Connecticut, in Hillsdale."

"Let's see, your representative would be Jane Featherington. I can put you through to her private extension."

"Uh, what if I didn't want to work with Jane? Who else would you suggest?"

"Sir, I'm sorry, but our cosmetics Sales Genies – that's what we call them because they deliver magic – our Sales Genies have exclusive territories. Jane is the only rep in your area."

"How many areas do you have in Connecticut?" I asked.

"Sir, if you're not interested in working with Jane then Kerry May isn't for you."

And with that, she was gone, genies be damned.

A few extra clicks on their website revealed what I needed to know. If I'd have done that first, I wouldn't have needed to disturb the woman on the phone who surely felt badly for hanging up on me. I discovered that Kerry May divided Connecticut into four territories. Jane had the largest, comprising New Haven and the eastern counties. The only phone number listed was the 888 one – apparently, they liked to keep their operation under tight control.

Jane's calendar showed a KM for that night at seven in East Haven. Probably canceled. But then, maybe not.

I brought Mary Ellen up to speed, hoping she'd be intrigued enough to go with me to the Kerry May party. Mary Ellen hasn't entirely signed off on this private eye enterprise, though I think she's okay with it if I keep my promise to avoid dangerous people, stay out of bars tailing spouses, and so on. And, of course, no gun. So I reasoned if I spun this right, she'd have no objection. And I was correct. But I had to go without her.

"We can't leave Stay alone. It's a new place for her. What if she heard a noise?" And to think I worried about her taking to the dog.

Mary Ellen briefed me on how these kinds of parties worked. A person hosts and gets a bunch of freebies in exchange for inviting her friends to attend and listen to sales pitches for the products. The fact I didn't know anyone might raise an eyebrow or two, but I could say my wife heard about it from someone and couldn't come. I didn't imagine there would be a problem as long as I brought my credit card.

And there wasn't. "I'm so sorry your wife fell and broke her shoulder, but I'll be right by your side telling you what she wants." Jane's replacement's name was Carla. Carla Keefer. I put her card in my pocket. "Please call me Carla," she'd said, and then sneezed loudly. "You must have a long-haired dog. I'm allergic, but I'll be okay. Excuse me. I need to take a little pill."

I bought some perfume, or Kerry Smell #2 as they called it, as soon as I could so Carla would back off and give me some space. The other women seemed nice enough, almost in a trance as they laser-focused on every product passed around. I think I could have taken my clothes off and sung "Danny Boy" and not been noticed – some people live to shop and buy stuff.

Around midway through the otherwise predictable event, Carla excused herself again, this time emerging from the kitchen carrying a huge canvas bag with wooden handles. It contained the evening's refreshments. And you guessed it: besides the usual crunchy things, there were several containers of vanilla-frosted cupcakes in lavender foils exactly like the one I pocketed in the parking lot near Jane's body. Honestly? They were great!

"Richard, I'm so glad you bought some Kerry Smell #2 for your wife. Wait till you see what we have to offer in the feminine spray line. She'll thank you forever if you buy Kerry Fresh for her. Everyone is talking about it."

God, I hoped not.

"So, Carla," I began. What's with the yummy cupcakes? Are they Kerry May products, too? Perhaps Kerry Kupcakes with a 'K'?"

"Richard, that's an incredible idea. I'll have to check into that. But, no, the cupcakes are my contribution to Kerry May events. I provided them to the three other women who sell Kerry May in Connecticut. Because I live closest to White Plains, I pick up the products, and the women come to me for whatever they need. I receive a little extra from the company for doing this, and I pass on my gratitude to the women. But, I must say, compliments like yours may drive me to market them."

"Lavender, I'm guessing, is the Kerry May signature color, huh?" I asked, reaching for my fourth cupcake. Okay, fifth.

"Yes, lavender. Isn't that cool? You know lavender has mystical properties, just like

Kerry May products. Would you believe these cupcake foils that I found at Michael's match Kerry May's patented lavender almost perfectly?"

"It's interesting because I saw a lavender car recently," I said. "I don't think I've ever seen a lavender car. Closest was mauve in the eighties."

"Richard, I can assure you that if you saw a lavender car – a lavender Lexus – you saw a one of a kind, and it must have belonged to the late Jane Featherington, may she rest in peace. Kerry May has a deal with Lexus. They make lavender cars exclusively for us. Only the top saleswomen are entitled to drive one. Poor Jane has been the New England star for the last two years. Someday I'm hoping I'll be so worthy."

When Carla's back was turned, I punched a few numbers on my iPhone and made it ring my church bell chime ring. I pretend-answered it and said I'd be right there.

"I'm sorry you have to leave, Richard, but here's a flyer with some future parties. Guess I'll be taking over Jane's territory. Poor Jane. Anyway, do come again if your wife wants something else. I'm truly sorry you'll miss the

Kerry Fresh demonstration, er, presentation – you know what I mean."

It must have been all the Kerry May Kupcakes because I now had one of my strong hunches combined with an inkling of what to do. If it turned out the foil or crumbs from the one I'd recovered in the parking lot tested positively for some kind of drug or poison I could, of course, go to the police, and I would if I had to, but admitting I'd pilfered evidence from a crime scene would end my PI career. So what would normally be Plan A slipped down to Plan B. Besides, my new Plan A would be much more interesting.

I awoke early the next morning to Stay staring me in the face. That she had learned in only a few days not to jump on the bed with Mary Ellen and me was testimony to some inner discipline that I'd not observed with food. Still, *her* Plan B was equally as effective: breathing her dog breath within an inch of my nose woke me up immediately.

Stay made an initial rush at some mourning doves in the bushes who were scrounging around for whatever mourning doves scrounge around for, but was quick with her constitutional and soon inside to await her breakfast. She initially sniffed at her BLUE

Buffalo Wilderness, apparently recalling yesterday when I'd tossed her a few cold hot dogs. But after watching me make coffee and begin my oatmeal, she forgot her protest and scarfed down the commercial fare, with an occasional lifted eyebrow to remind me I was a great disappointment to her.

I rinsed out my cereal bowl, carried my coffee to the study, and called Matt. "Say, I wanted to have something analyzed chemically, how would I go about it?"

"Dad, you'd have to take it to a commercial laboratory, tell them what you're looking for, and pay whatever they asked. It could be pretty expensive, and takes a long time at most places. Unless someone important declared it an emergency."

"No, no. Nothing like that. Just curious."

"Dad, what's going on? Does this have to do with your private eye job?"

So I told him the whole story. Matt is the kindest, smartest son anyone could want. And, did I say smart? His work for one of the alphabet soup spy agencies in Washington is top secret. Since he's a computer genius, I've always suspected that what he does a lot of is hacking bad guys or bad countries. I've never asked him directly, but it has to be something like that.

"Dad, I can have the foils analyzed if you FedEx them to me. If this Jane ate anything that caused her death so suddenly without lots of vomiting and other messy bodily fluids, then it almost certainly would have to have been laced with cyanide."

"Cyanide? Where would you buy cyanide?" I asked.

"You can't legally, unless you're a government or university lab with good reasons. But, that doesn't mean you can't get it – either the chemicals to make it or the pills that you hear about spies popping when they're captured. In fact, I'd bet I could buy some with a few clicks of my mouse. The Internet is still in its wild west phase."

"But wouldn't cyanide have turned up in the coroner's exam?" I asked.

"Not if they weren't screening for it. Its half-life in the blood is an hour, tops. Could be detected in the hair or tissues, but a routine autopsy would seldom go that far."

Now using tweezers, I put the cupcake foil with its few crumbs still clinging to it into an envelope. I dropped it off at the FedEx office in New Haven, paying for overnight delivery. I texted Matt and reminded him of precautions necessary on his end, but being a spy of some kind, he likely smiled at my caution. Of course, I had no idea if cyanide lasted as long on aluminum or in crumbs as it was supposed to in hair or tissues, but it was worth a shot.

I returned home to a note informing me that Mary Ellen had taken Stay to church with her. Although I was no longer the pastor of the Hillsdale Community Church, Mary Ellen continued her active role with the food pantry while I merely attended on Sundays. My current roost was the back row on the aisle where I sat trying not to roll my eyes at the new preacher's simplistic sermons. For the life of me, I couldn't figure out why attendance had grown so rapidly since my departure a few months ago.

After my presence at the Kerry May party, I was now on what seemed to be an hourly email blast. "Help me win the Lexus," were her imbedded parting words on each. The next party was scheduled tomorrow evening in Willimantic, another home on Jane's schedule. I would go. I would go even though it was highly unlikely Matt's lab would have finished with the analysis. I would go and I would confront Carla. And I would hope I was right. I would also go as a woman.

As you may remember, I seldom need to shave, so I wasn't worried that my facial features would betray me. Hair, though, was my Achilles' heel, so to speak. The private eye school I'd attended, and from which I'd graduated with honors, said that wigs always made for good disguises.

Harris Street Hair in New Haven seemed the nearest, most logical place to begin my shopping. "I'm interested in a wig," I said to the 60ish man who welcomed me.

"Sir, we supply hair assistance only to women. May I recommend that you visit Tomas' Toupees for your needs?"

"No, you don't understand. I want a woman's wig for me."

"Oh, I see," he said. "Another one of those."

He and I clearly would never be on the same page regarding gender issues, but I chose not to enter debate mode. "Yes," I said, "one of those."

I tried on a few and settled on a blonde one with wavy ends, sort of a Farrah Fawcett touch, it seemed to me. The mirror revealed a not entirely unattractive woman, at least from the neck up.

Wending my way out of New Haven, I decided JC Penney at the Valley Mall would be my next stop. A wig plus absence of a beard would obviously not be enough. I needed something for a top shelf.

I'd never bought a bra before. Probably most men haven't, but I wouldn't know for sure because the matter doesn't come up in normal conversation among guys. "Say, how about those Red Sox!" "Right, what a team! And did you know Penney's is having a sale on bras?"

Penney's "Push 'em up bras" had their own corner in the women's intimate department. I wanted to get in and out as fast as I could, but I didn't know what size to buy besides "pretty big." But not too big, of course, because I didn't want the contraption falling down around my waist. I'd settled on a "Full-Figure Two Girls Up" model in size 46 when a saleswoman, 70 or so, approached.

"May I help you, sir? Looking for a good time?"

"Excuse me?" I said, stunned.

"What's the matter, hard of hearing? I said are you looking in the right line?"

Thank the Lord. Mary Ellen was right. I was missing consonants more and more often. If I didn't have my hearing checked soon, it was going to get me in trouble.

"I don't know, my wife, uh, is a largish woman, you know what I mean, and I'd like to surprise her with a little something."

"Well, sonny, these Two Girls Up bras are not little somethings. But they will keep the damn things out of her lap."

I settled on a black one. I figured some wash cloths or hand towels should fill the cups nicely. I stopped by the "Dress for Success" department, added a blazer, blouse and extra-long pants and departed. I would wear my black Rockports, which were gender neutral.

As luck would have it, I didn't need to make up an excuse to leave the house the night of the party. Mary Ellen received a last-minute call from daughter Lucy to join her at Nordstrom's for a light dinner and some shopping. So I left a note – "Gone out, be back later." She was used to my frequent, sudden departures from when I was a minister so I didn't think she'd worry. Stay secured her place in the Outback's command post behind me and, following a brief stop at Petco for a couple of items, we were on our way.

As before, the only password I needed to enter the Kerry May shebang was "I heard about it." While I must say I was confident I could pass for a woman visually, I also knew I absolutely had to mind my voice. A tenor, I had a habit of dropping my voice to a lower register at the end of sentences, something that earned me no little criticism as a public speaker. I'd practiced on the hour drive from Hillsdale, much to Stay's consternation. "How are you, Stay?" I asked in a falsetto. Stay initially glanced around to see who might be addressing her. She finally bet on the source coming from under the right front seat. I had to reach back and push her away to keep her from digging through the bottom of the car. That's when she got an eyeful of my blondeness. A couple of barks plus a leaping attempt to grab the wig let me know her opinion.

Stay was also not happy with being ordered to "sit" in the car, which I commanded upon arrival in Willimantic. Jane must have been the genius behind teaching Stay to stay when she said, "sit." Of course, Stay usually sat when she stayed anyway, so I wasn't sure what pedagogical method she'd used. Whatever. It worked.

157

Funny, but with all the brain power going into my strategy, I'd neglected to think of an alias. "My name is, uh, uh, … Bertha," I stammered upon entering.

"Well, Uh, Uh, Bertha, Nancy, the hostess, and I are certainly glad you've come tonight," Carla said, her perfume clogging the air between us. "And I think we have something that might interest you."

I was aware that at six feet tall and heavier than I ought to be, I was an imposing, if not stare-worthy physical female specimen. Which was why I figured Carla led me to a table filled with Kerry Dry, what they call their antiperspirant line. Carla, who was no twig herself, said, "We plus sizes need all the help we can get."

"Yes," I modulated higher than necessary, "we do."

I chose a Queen Anne chair in which to sit. I had rehearsed in my head how I would stage the confrontation, my first maneuver requiring me to get directly in Carla's face, hence needing a good base from which to leap. But, as with so many plans, it didn't come off as designed.

"Dear," said a woman about my age sitting to my right, "my name's Ann. I think you're having slippage issues."

I grabbed my chest/breasts and realized the towel I'd stuffed in one of the cups was no longer there. The other was holding up fine, but, they don't call my bra "Two Girls" for nothing. So there I sat with one half pointing to the ceiling and the other reduced to a lumpy, lost sister. Still, I didn't think anyone would notice as long as I remained seated. I mean, everyone was there for Kerry May, not to stare at my breasts. Right?

Wrong. "Look, her boob has expired!" Ann bellowed.

Carla jumped to my aide. "Ann! How dare you talk about Bertha like that! We've all had our little or big problems like this." She was on the verge of continuing, but began sniffling and then sneezed. And then sneezed again. And then again.

"Goodness," Carla said. "I haven't sneezed like this since, I don't know, the other night. You must have a long-haired dog. Say, were you at my party dressed as a man?"

"Yes," I said, in my natural tenor voice. "I mean no, I wasn't dressed as a man. Or, yes, I was. And, yes, I was at your party. As a man.

As the man I am. As the man I gladly am."
And with this bold affirmation of gender, I
reached under my blazer and blouse and tried
to rid myself of my intimate apparel, which
suddenly felt like something feral loose in my
midsection. I came out with the deflated cup,
but the other remained proud, albeit aiming
lower. As if on cue, the lifetime guaranteed
elastic yanked everything out of my hand,
leaving me with what could only be called a
"unique" presentation.

"What in heaven's name is going on?"
Carla cried. I think another woman shrieked
also, but to the credit of the rest, they were not
being deterred from their charge to check out
the Kerry May products being passed around.
A man/woman with a hanging brassiere was
no competition in the least.

Although absolutely nothing so far was
going according to script, it was time to
execute what remained of my scheme. I
reached into my pocket, extracted the Petco
dog whistle, and gave it a blow. Within
seconds, there was scratching at the door.

"Who could that be?" inquired Nancy the
hostess, who swung open the door with a
smile on her face. Stay rushed in, immediately
went to the refreshment table, and began

sampling the fare as fast as she could. I'm sure she thought she was in doggy heaven.

"Get that dog out of here!" shouted Carla, who promptly began sneezing, one explosion after the other. "Stay! Stay! You hear me, you stupid dog? Stay!"

And you know what Stay did, hearing herself called multiple times. She was soon jumping up and down on Carla, who was backing towards the kitchen, fending off Stay with one hand and using napkins to cover her exploding nose with the other.

Stay, meanwhile, had identified her as the source of the cupcakes and finger sandwiches, not to mention the cheese and crackers, and decided that this woman who kept calling her would only lead her to even better snacks. In fact, now armed with a cupcake in one hand, Carla was luring Stay to the front door, which she opened. Tossing the lavender delight onto the front porch, she didn't have to tell Stay to fetch. The dog was gone. Carla slammed the door.

Despite hanging out in an unbecoming way, I stood, flashed my plastic police badge, another recommendation from college I'd used successfully in Arizona, and as quickly put it away. "Carla, you're under arrest for the murder of Jane Featherington."

Even the women hovering over the table full of Kerry May goodies gave me their undivided attention. You could have heard a pin drop except for the yelling of "What? Are you nuts?" by, I think, everyone in the room.

"You, sir, are deranged," Carla declared, and came at me with fury in her eyes and a pair of ice tongs in her hand. She poked me in my chest that, thank God, was still well padded, but her rush did put me on my keister. "Sit on him, Martha. You too, June. I'm calling the police."

With 400 pounds of Kerry May–crazed women on top of me, I still managed to maneuver the arm with the hand holding the dog whistle to my lips and blow. More door scratching.

"I wonder who that is," declared Nancy, who seemed to be the only one who hadn't figured out that this was not a normal Kerry May party.

This time the door was barely open when at least a half dozen dogs led by Stay burst into the room. As you'd imagine, Carla was quite undone. Not because I'm a minister at heart, but one must take a certain pity on someone who can't stop sneezing and who is dripping with snot. So I indulged myself with a moment of sympathy.

Reaching into her giant bag, Carla came up with a cupcake that appeared like all the others except with chocolate frosting. "Come here, doggie," she was saying to Stay. "I bet you go with big Bertha, the sexually confused person, don't you?" Stay would have agreed to anything at that point. "Well, let's just see how you like this cupcake, big girl."

"Carla, wait. Don't do it. I'll leave. Okay?" I was as frantic as a person who was being squashed could be.

But it was too late. Never one to tarry over a meal, Stay leaped and grabbed the cake from Carla's hand. The other dogs looked on with envy.

I had to get to Stay. I tried again to push the heavyweights off, but to no avail. Then the doorbell rang. Couldn't have been Stay this time.

"I wonder who that is," Nancy asked, revealing without a doubt that she must have sniffed way more than her share of Kerry May products over the years.

"Someone here call the police?" a young Willimantic cop asked. "I'm Officer Cortez.

What's going on? Why is that woman in the bad wig underneath the fat women? What kind of kinky games are you people playing?"

"Officer, arrest that woman or man. He brought his dogs and tried to attack us. I'm a Kerry May Sales Genie, and this is my Kerry May party. Nancy is the homeowner. And we want him out of here, don't we, Nancy?" Carla then proceeded to have a sneezing fit.

After convincing Martha and June that they could safely attempt to get to their feet from atop my breathless form, Officer Cortez pulled me up. For the first time, Nancy seemed aware of her environment, as they say in psychiatric intake evaluations. Still, putting together the mental contradiction of Kerry May and police presence wasn't helping her make a decision about what to do with me. Before she could attempt a guess at the right answer, I dashed for the kitchen. Officer Cortez followed, "Where are you going? Stay right there! Stay! Or I'll tase you!"

And there was Stay. Curled up. With an uneaten cupcake at her feet. Talk about having good taste. Or rather good smell. I would later learn that while only a small percentage of people can detect the almond scent in cyanide, most animals can. And Stay was some kind of animal!

Just hearing her name shouted, however innocently by Officer Cortez, awakened her. She sniffed at the cupcake one more time to make sure it was something she didn't want, came to me to see if I needed her, and then trotted off to the living room to join the other dogs in enjoying the remaining treats on the table.

My phone buzzed. I reached into my pocket. Officer Cortez assumed an aggressive stance. "Don't go there!" he exclaimed.

"It's my phone," I said. "It's just my phone."

"It can wait. Now sit down in that chair. Ma'am, you said the dogs attacked you?"

"Yes. Especially the golden retriever." Carla blew her nose. "That dog is a killer."

"How did they attack you?"

"He knows I'm allergic to dogs, and he brought in a bunch of them to distract me and steal my Kerry May products."

With the officer engaged with Carla the sneezer, I stole a peek at my phone. A text. "Cyanide confirmed. Love, Matt."

"Officer Cortez, I'm a private investigator. And–"

"May I see your Private ID?"

"Well, that's just it, I don't have any, I'm probationary, should be in the mail any day. Anyway, I've just confirmed that this woman poisoned another Kerry May Sales Genie with cyanide. And also tried to poison my dog with that cupcake over there."

While I was talking, Carla had edged towards the dining room and then made a dash for her canvas bag. She pulled out a cupcake and declared, "As they say in the B movies – Copper, you'll never take me alive." And with that, she bit into the cupcake.

And, then, making a face, she said, "Oh, crap. That was the wrong cupcake." But by this time, Officer Cortez had pinned her arms behind her and begun fitting her wrists with cuffs.

"It's not fair," she said. "All I wanted was a luxurious, lavish, lavender Lexus. And it was going to be mine. It's not fair. It's just not fair." And then she sneezed.

***

"Richard, you know I should write you up and have your provisional license taken away, don't you?" Bob said.

I was contrite – I knew I'd done wrong. But I was also relieved – the criminal had been arrested, and Stay was safe. And I was also no little bit proud: I'd outsmarted everyone when it counted. I would have made a heck of a PI if I hadn't blown it on my first sort-of case. "Bob, do what you have to do. But don't forget: we're not having this conversation if I didn't pick up the cupcake foil, are we?"

"No. But don't think I didn't see it. I did. I made a note of it. To tell the mall owner to do a better job of picking up his litter. Ignore litter today, and tomorrow you'll have a serial killer. I've seen it before. On *NYPD* I think it was."

"So, what's the verdict?"

"Oh, don't worry about it. Only problem is somehow we have to find Myron and get him in on it to take the credit. If he says you were there because he assigned you, then we're all good to go. Of course, Jane's sister will need to swear she hired both of you, but I'm sure she'll give you much more than that for a reward."

"Say, did you ever meet my dog, Stay?" I whistled, and pictured the golden beauty slipping out the rear passenger window to come find her beloved master.

"Bob, this is Stay. Stay, this is Bob."

Stay lifted a paw and Bob reached for it. Both sneezed.

The End

Some Kind of Affair

I'd just peeled back the tab of my Dunkin' Donuts coffee in anxious anticipation of my first cup of morning java when a knock on the door of my strip mall private detective office was followed by the entrance of my younger sister, Robin. Since we'd seen each other a couple of days earlier, my first thought, of course, was that something terrible had happened. It had.

"John is having an affair, I know it," she said, before plopping down in one of my IKEA chairs. "I didn't want to admit it for the longest time, but now I can't deny it. Can you find out for me?"

John Grogan and Robin have been married five years. He's an orthopedic surgeon and part-time medical director of the Oak Lawn Nursing and Rehabilitation Center in New Haven. An odd guy in a thoroughly brilliant sort of way, John met Robin when he patronized the women's clothing store that Robin manages. He was looking for a velvet dress for his mother. Apparently, it was the gentle manner in which Robin broke the news to him that velvet was no longer in vogue that won his heart. He'd invited her on the spot to a concert, and Cupid took it from there. What Cupid didn't know, however, was how close John was to his mother, Irene. Robin once said that they were never alone because she always felt Irene's presence in the room. Last I heard, though, they'd worked through that with some counseling. Still, I couldn't imagine anyone more unlikely to have an affair than John.

"Robin, are we talking about *your* John?" I said, handing her a box of tissues. "What on earth makes you think John's cheating on you?"

"John is always receiving phone calls related to his practice, so I'm used to that. He answers a few questions and either ends it by saying he'll be right there or asking them to make an appointment. But lately he gets calls at odd hours and always steps out of the room. And the conversations never last more than fifteen, thirty seconds. And when I ask who it was, he says not to worry about it. And now he texts. John never texted before in his life. And his work hours are longer. He's only paid to spend a day or so at Oak Lawn, but this last week I know he went there five times. Then there's this black beret he wears. All the time. I mean all the time! At night too, for all I know since we have separate bedrooms. Never takes it off. Something's really funny, Richard, and I hate to bother you with this, but I don't know what else to do, who else to turn to."

"Of course I'll help," I said. I mean it wasn't as if I had a busy life – my practice was still in its infancy, by which I mean barely crawling. I'd counted on word of mouth for advertising, but I was learning it's hard to get one mouth to talk to another if there is no first mouth to start with. Well, I did have one successful case, having solved the lavender Lexus mystery, but I'd had to share the spotlight with Myron who, since I'm apprenticed to him, technically took credit for the collar of the murderous Kerry May Sales Genie. In any event, I had plenty of time to give to my sister and her suspicion.

"You'll need to give me John's usual routine," I said. "I'll have to figure out a disguise and rent a car to tail him so he won't make me."

"I'm good for the money, whatever it takes," my little sister said. She also knew that thanks to my wife Mary Ellen's inheritance I needed more money like the Kardashian sisters needed more attention. My new life was solely for thrills.

"Don't worry about that," I said. "If I need to, I can also rustle up some electronic devices for his car, maybe his phone, too. But first, I'll do the basic Tailing 101. I'm going to bet there's a reason for his behavior because, let's face it, Robin, John is not your normal doctor, not even your normal person."

Come to think of it, John probably was a bona fide, Mensa-certifiable genius, an untidy, disorganized scientific type with far-ranging interests. He also trusted his instincts far too much. Before he met Robin, he self-published a diet book. He'd become convinced that a prune diet would not only cleanse one's body of toxins but also improve one's immune system. Such hadn't been proven in a lab, of course – that would be a waste of time, he reasoned. To say the least, John was more than a little arrogant.

His book sold very well after Dr. Oz had him on his show. But then the prune industry brought litigation. You'd think the prune people would be happy about selling all those prunes, but apparently they're regular people who didn't want their fruit connected to what many deemed a scam. John and the prune people settled out of court.

Then there was the time, shortly after their wedding, that I opened the *New Haven Register* one day to read that John had been removed from his position of treasurer of the state medical association. Seems he invested some of the association's money along with his own in a surefire exercise equipment venture, the EZ CorePower Belt, which he'd learned about on the Internet. The belt had pockets that you filled with variable amounts of lead weight, depending on your goal. The theory was that wearing this belt every day would require the wearer to keep abdominal and back muscles in a state of constant rigor. Good looks and good health could only result, right? I mean, what could go wrong? Well, what went wrong was a bunch of people who overloaded either their front or their back and fell down, with some not being able to stand up without taking off the belt. One guy – I guess the one who led the class action suit – hit the deck while giving a presentation at his firm before his superiors. When he tried to stand up, he unfortunately left his pants on the floor. Another out-of-court settlement and a resignation from the medical society followed.

So, no, John may be a great doctor, but he's not typical in any way.

"I know," Robin said, "but he's always been so loving and attentive and now he's clearly preoccupied with someone. I can't stand it. Thank goodness we don't have children."

After Robin left, I headed back to the Dunkin' Donuts in Cheshire, a place where I'd learned over the years I do my best thinking.

"Hey, Reverend, what's happening?" Rhonda welcomed me as soon as I entered. "Usual?"

"Morning, Rhonda. Yup. How's that beautiful young lady of yours?" Kaitlin, Rhonda's then three-month-old daughter, was the last child I'd baptized before retiring from the Hillsdale Community Church. That Sunday had been a very special day.

"She's cutting some teeth. Not going to be an easy day for Grandma. Is Stay in the car?"

Stay was my golden retriever, an unexpected bonus from the Featherington case. Even I didn't like donuts more than Stay, who frequently accompanied me to dining opportunities at Dunkin'.

"She's with her grandma, too, but don't tell Mary Ellen I called her that. They're enjoying the day on the Rails to Trails pathway." Mary Ellen's the runner in our family, and Stay loves to go with her.

After Rhonda gave me my coffee and two glazed donut sticks, she waited on the next customer and I found a table. Time for some deep cogitation. Following someone wasn't hard. Worst part was the long hours of doing nothing interrupted by bursts of doing a lot. There's no rhythm to the day. Biggest problem in this case was that John knew me. Although I'd had good luck with a woman's wig in previous surveillance experiences, my last one involving the embarrassing attempt to include a top shelf made me skittish about portraying a woman again any time soon. So a man I would have to be.

After an hour of watching customers come and go while I plotted, I ordered a coffee refill for the road, bid farewell to Rhonda, and drove my Outback to New Haven and Tomas' Toupees. Half an hour later, I left with a straggly beard and a cool, vintage 50s ducktail hairpiece.

As you may know, Udriveme Car Rental will pick you up, and they did after I stored my Outback in the garage. Lunchtime was fast approaching, and I wondered if I'd missed the chance to tail John from his office to wherever he goes for lunch, assuming he went out at all. Robin hadn't yet given me his schedule, but noon is noon, so nothing ventured, nothing gained.

I parked the rental Corolla in the farthest reach of the parking lot of John's office. His Mercedes coupe was in its usual place. As I'd learned in my private eye college course, I was tempted to walk over and touch the hood to see if it was warm from a recent drive. But that would mean putting on my scratchy beard and hair disguise, something I hoped to delay as long as possible.

I'd about concluded that I'd missed John's lunch foray when he emerged from the building and jumped into his car. A brief sojourn down the road led to a left turn into the Soundview Shopping Center, signaling to me a lunch at either Panera Bread or Chipotle Mexican Grill. So imagine my surprise when he chose instead the post office and was in and out in a couple of minutes bearing a brown-wrapped package. The traffic lights on the main drag made keeping up with John a challenge, but nothing I couldn't handle. After all, he didn't know my car, and now wearing my disguise, I could ride his bumper at will.

When he turned into the Oak Lawn Nursing and Rehabilitation Center, however, I chose to pass by the entrance. Following a series of turns, I doubled back and parked first in "Clergy Parking" by habit before catching myself and redirecting my Corolla to the visitors' lot. About half of Oak Lawn's 100 or so patients would be there until they left feet first, while the others were short-termers working their way back from hip or knee replacements or the like. As Rev. Burgess, I was known to many of the staff, but especially to Barbara, the head of nursing. As Richard the private eye wearing a beard and ducktails, I was just another odd-looking man.

I didn't know all the details of John's duties at Oak Lawn. I presumed that as its part-time medical director, he functioned in some oversight capacity authorizing certain kinds of prescriptions, maybe approving admissions, discharges, and so on. Robin had said she knew he'd been spending more time there than usual, but I had no idea whether that had to do with medicine or a certain someone. I had to work from the inside to determine that.

My disguise caused more than a few heads to turn as I wandered down first one hallway, then another. I tried not to peer into people's rooms, a rude behavior no clergy person would ever indulge in. My peripheral vision, though, is good enough that I relied on it to tell me if someone was standing or moving in the rooms. If there was, a quick glance sufficed, usually undetected. Of course, I also listened for John's voice, a pitch and timbre all its own.

I found him in one of the center's semi-private rooms still wearing his beret. I wished I could be in the room to observe more closely. A supply closet a few doors down gave me an idea. I'd hoped to find a bucket and a mop but hit the jackpot with a gallery of coveralls in addition. In short order, my chest said I was Roger. With the bucket filled with water and the mop, I left to eavesdrop on John. But I never got there.

"Hey, you, Roger is it? Can you go down to Room 48? Evelyn poured her pitcher full of water into the artificial fern again – there's water all over the floor."

I was trapped. I couldn't very well decline without setting off a firestorm and ruining possibilities for later visits. So I went to Evelyn's room to see about her fern issue.

Evelyn, mercifully, was deep asleep, the puddles on the floor no problem even for my untrained janitorial abilities. Since hers was one of the private rooms in the place, I had no other company. However, it was definitely time for Roger to leave. But how? The windows were too small, and surely locked besides. I could venture back down the hallway, but that would take me past the nurses' station. Or, I could pull the fire alarm I'd seen outside Evelyn's door.

Sirens blared, lights flashed, doors began closing mysteriously. But not before I'd dashed through the running throng of health care workers to the safety of my car. I couldn't peel out of there fast enough. I hoped Roger would have a good explanation for the mess he'd left behind when he showed up.

I arrived home right behind Mary Ellen. Stay leaped out of the Mini Cooper in which she more than takes up the back seat and ran to greet me. I could tell from Stay's enthusiasm that she was dying to tell me something: "Daddy! Daddy! You know what happened?" she seemed to say.

Instead, it was Mary Ellen. "Dickie, Dickie, you know what happened?" My answer being no, my wife continued, "We were running along and heard shouting and screaming. Then barking. Stay pulled the leash out of my hand,

and by the time I caught up to her she'd chased away a coyote that had cornered this little dog. The owner, a young woman named Ann, was hysterical. She said the coyote had come out of nowhere, nipped at her dog, and pursued it into the woods and back. Stay broke the chase up and scared the coyote away. Aren't you proud of her?"

"Good girl! Good girl!" Stay rolled on her back, all four paws in the air, letting me rub her tummy. "You're a good girl, Stay, a hero, er, heroine. I'm so proud of you!" She let me stroke her a few more times before turning over, jumping up, snorting for whatever reasons dogs snort, and making a dash for the kitchen. Stay had already learned that in our house whenever you do good (or really most anything that isn't bad) you're rewarded with food. Pushing her aside with my foot so I could open the refrigerator door, I slipped a couple of turkey franks from the package and tossed them to her. She caught both and scampered to the corner where, now safe from a predator who might want to steal her weenies, she proceeded to swallow them, mostly whole. "That's all, girl, there's always tomorrow." Disappointment spread over Stay's face, but I knew she'd get over it.

I decided to take the rest of the hot dogs and do some grilling. My morning donuts had long outlived their usefulness, and the adrenaline rush of the nursing home experience had been surmounted. In fact, I was famished. Mary Ellen rustled up a salad and fixings and we chose our usual chairs around the white wrought-iron table. I brought Mary Ellen up to speed on my new case. Like me, she found it hard to fathom John having an affair with a woman or man or any other living thing. "So what are you going to do next?" she asked. "I hope you're not going back to the nursing home."

"I'm not smart enough to know much else to do other than shadow John again tomorrow," I said. "Maybe another hot dog will help me think."

I could not have known then that the answer to my prayers was in the works even as we spoke.

Like I planned, I'd followed John again the next day. Same routine – his office, post office with package, Oak Lawn. He was in Oak Lawn for about an hour. Then back to his office and later home. Dullsville.

After dinner, while mulling over another tack and scratching Stay's ears for inspiration, the phone rang. "Barry Roeder," Mary Ellen announced on her way back from the kitchen. Rev. Barry Roeder is the person who succeeded me as the minister of the Hillsdale Community Church. We have a cordial relationship, one that I try to nurture, mostly by staying out of his way. The church is his gig now, and that's fine with me.

"Richard, I need your help. You know Arthur, the retired dentist? Well, he's become a huge problem for me same as he was for you."

I remembered Arthur all too well. After he left his practice, Arthur never missed church. Unfortunately. Rare was the announcement period midway through the service that he didn't stand up and take issue with the sermon that had just concluded. At first, people were amused. Then upset. Then irate. Complicating the matter was the fact that his pledge to the church was ten per cent of the budget. We reckoned we'd cut him off at the pass by moving the announcement time to the beginning of the service. Didn't help. He came prepared to comment on the previous week's sermon. Needless to say, not having Arthur to deal with helped mitigate any doubt I might have had about retiring early.

Barry had come up with an ingenious ploy, I thought – he omitted printed bulletins and verbal announcements entirely in favor of projecting everything necessary to good worship on a screen in the front. And that worked for a while. But Barry made a mistake. In his enthusiasm to move to a "total digital experience," he soon coupled his projection experiment with a Twitter "ministry." People were encouraged to tweet their comments and questions during the service, which also were projected for all to see. Since Arthur had a reputation for being technologically phobic, it sounded like a plan, right? Wrong. Arthur bought an iPhone, involved his grandchildren as instructors, and became a compulsive tweeter. Including during the sermons. "That's bull!" was one tweet flashed for all to see. "You're the worst preacher we ever had," was another. Recently, he had taken to scouring the internet during the choir's anthems and tweeting his findings: "Ronald Reagan is alive and well, says Globe."

"The crazy part is," Barry was saying, "Arthur now declares you were the greatest pastor ever. He can't stop talking about you, says letting you retire was the stupidest thing the church ever did. Anyway, Arthur fell and broke his hip and is recuperating at Oak Lawn. He's asking for you. Would you go see him as a favor to me?"

Yesterday I would have said, "Hell, no." Today, I said, "I'd be delighted."

I wasn't sure how I'd work Arthur into my surveillance strategy, but the nursing home portion would certainly be easier as Richard the pastor than as a scraggly bearded guy. While there, I also intended to ask Head Nurse Barbara a few questions about Dr. John. Doctors may make all the money, but if it's help you need, see a nurse.

I thought I might be on to a significant development when John left his office the next morning around 10 and scurried away in his Mercedes. I choked back the rest of my donut and pulled out in pursuit. Turns out I could have enjoyed my treat more leisurely as John's destination was the local CVS. He was in and out within a couple of minutes toting a small bag – a prescription, batteries, Preparation H, who knows. He returned to his building, and so did I.

As in days past, his first afternoon stop was the post office. And, no surprise, Oak Lawn was next. I threw my disguise into the back and waltzed in as if to visit a parishioner, an honest pursuit that seemed oddly strange after my life of lies in recent weeks as a detective. I saw him enter his office suite to the left, the same place we'd met a few years back to confer about a patient. His suite contained an outer office with a few chairs and another office, his private one, in the back. He placed his now familiar brown package from the post office on a table in the first office and entered the second. I waited a few more moments without John emerging and decided to find Arthur.

Arthur was fully dressed in the bed by the window, asleep on top of the bedspread, a classic position for people who've recently returned exhausted from physical therapy in rehab centers. I'd noticed his roommate in the hall on my previous visit – a man in his early sixties sitting in his chair watching television on a little set attached to the wall by an adjustable arm mechanism. He'd caught my attention because of his strange hair pattern, though I'm not sure that's the word to use. Tufts, or better, clumps of matted, thick red hair protruded seemingly at random on his head. A whiteboard opposite his bed declared his name, Robert Swafford, with a reminder that today was Thursday and his nurse was Stephanie.

"Good afternoon, Robert, or do you prefer to be called Bob?" I said.

"Bob is fine. Who are you?"

"I'm a friend of Arthur's over there, his former pastor. How are you doing?"

Bob began coughing, hacking in an odd way. I wondered if he might have an upper respiratory infection. Catching his wind, he focused on me, his tongue lolling out of his mouth more than most people's do, and scratched his right ear with the back of his hand. "Want a cookie?" Bob offered with the same ear-scratching hand. "They're terrific."

"No, thanks, watching my weight. You been here long?"

"Couple weeks. Hoping to go home tomorrow. Whoopee, ah-oo!" His understandable exuberance included a shrill, upper register sound. Again, he did the tongue deal, though he didn't scratch his ear.

Arthur stirred. "Reverend Burgess? To what do I owe this honor?"

"I'm helping out Pastor Roeder, wanted to see my old friend. How's the hip?" I chose a chair and pulled it close to Arthur.

"Good, good, but I'll tell you the physical therapy sucks big time. They aren't happy unless you're crying with pain. If I'd treated my patients like this, I wouldn't have had any patients. They're cruel, mean people, those therapists."

Bob had turned down his TV set, the better to overhear our conversation. "When is your daughter coming with her cat?" he asked Arthur. Arthur's daughter, Pam, had been the subject of a *New Haven Register* article recently for visiting children with her therapy cat, Midnight. I assumed from Bob's question that she must have brought it with her to see her dad.

"I don't know, Bob. I doubt she'll bring it again after yesterday. What the hell got into you, anyway?"

"Whaddya mean?" Bob replied.

"I mean your chasing that poor cat. You traumatized it something awful. What's your problem, anyway?"

I looked to Bob for an answer, but saw only a face that suggested shame with downcast, occasionally flitting eyes, and droopy mouth.

The rest of my visit with Arthur was unremarkable. He said nothing about the new pastor or our previous run-ins. I told him I'd return in a few days.

Barbara, the head nurse, was walking towards the entrance, it then being 3 PM and the end of her usual shift.

"Nice to see you visiting patients again," she said. "How's Mary Ellen?"

"She's good, we're good, loving retirement," I replied. "Say, I just ran into my brother-in-law, John. Hadn't seen him in several months. He doesn't seem himself," I lied, "what do you think?"

"Oh, I can't say I've noticed anything different about him except that he seems to be here more than usual. Oh, and his new cap. The patients love it. Says it gives him a French air. They also love the cookies he brings. They must be great, haven't had any myself."

I was on the verge of a second question, when a woman pushing a walker halted near us, semi-squatted, and relieved herself on the floor.

"Velma! That's the second time you did that today! Have you lost your mind?"

To Velma's credit, she spun her chariot around and headed off with nary a hint of regret.

"Amy, would you help me with Velma," Barbara hollered into another room. "She peed on the floor again."

Amy and Barbara hurried after Velma, who was really motoring with her walker. I followed at a safe distance, not wanting to become involved with female troubles or whatever was going on. When I believed she'd been redressed, I allowed myself to peek into Velma's room as the two nurses tried to help her into bed. They were having trouble because Velma was insisting on twirling around before she settled down. I also couldn't help but notice, now that I had a good view of Velma – she was growing a large patch of thick, matted hair on the back of her head just like Bob's.

Having succeeded at their task, Barbara joined me in a walk to the exit. "I can't tell you how many weird things our patients have been doing lately. Must be the full moon. Well, Richard, great to see you again. Don't be a stranger."

I hadn't seen John in any of my rounds so after bidding Barbara farewell I headed to his office to see if he was there. The outer door was open. I knocked on the inner one. No answer. Visiting his patients, of course. I pulled out one of my business cards with the intention to jot a note saying "let's have lunch sometime," but it slipped out of my hand and helicoptered behind me. That was when I saw the package underneath a chair. I stepped out of John's suite and inspected the hallway. No one except a few patients here and there, sitting outside their rooms for a change of scenery. I scooped up the package and beat a hasty retreat to my car.

Mary Ellen was dismayed at my thievery. "Dickie, that was an awful thing to do. He's going to accuse someone in the home of taking it." Obviously, I had fallen far from the moral paragon people considered me to be. But so had Mary Ellen who, without missing a beat, said, "well, since you have it, let's open it."

The return address was a Dr. Gordon Croft in St. John, New Brunswick, Canada. Since the package was identical to others I'd seen John picking up at the post office, I assumed the contents were the same also – cookies, exactly like Bob the ear-scratcher's, and no doubt the source of John's popularity at Oak Lawn. Dr. Croft must be a baker of some kind.

Or not. A Google search turned up a Gordon Croft, DVM, in St. John, New Brunswick – a veterinarian. Mary Ellen and I looked at each other, speechless. Stay had joined us but had taken one sniff of the cookies and headed for her L.L. Bean bed in the laundry room, a decision most out of character for our doggie.

"You're not going to eat one, are you?" Mary Ellen, asked, wide-eyed.

I said no, but I did. You may have noticed I have little willpower around food. The cookie was pretty good, a kind of snickerdoodle taste. I ate another to be sure it was as yummy as I thought it was. Oh, yes.

Why would a vet in Canada be sending cookies to a doctor in Connecticut? The most obvious answer would be that the vet has a hobby, maybe sells cookies on the side and John loves to make his patients happy. Case closed. But nothing's that simple. Besides, when a good mystery and food conspire, I can only give thanks for my new vocation.

My next detecting move was to check up on Velma – the little pee-maker. After dinner, Mary Ellen and Stay joined me in the Outback, Stay taking the command position right behind me. I explained to Mary Ellen the details of what I'd observed in the nursing home, but withheld my tentative conclusions for the time being. Stay wanted to join us as we got out of the car, but I gently pushed her inside. She let us know her feelings by turning her back on us and staring out the opposite window.

With the rush of activity in the afternoon, I'd necessarily abandoned my prior goal of stalking John for the day. I presumed he would be long gone from the hospital. Which was why I was surprised to literally bump into him on his way out.

"Pardon me! Richard! What are you doing here? Hello, Mary Ellen. Haven't seen you guys in ages. We should get together."

"Great idea, John," Mary Ellen answered. "Love your hat." Then, moving with all the quick-thinking dexterity of a world-class PI herself, she asked, "How about you and Robin coming over tomorrow night for a cookout? We'll pick up some steaks and Dickie can play chef."

"Sounds fun to me. I'll double-check with Robin. I'll be in touch. What brings you here?"

"I was asked to visit one of my former parishioners, Arthur Bentley," I said. "You know him?"

"The dentist. I met him briefly. He's a roommate of one of my patients, Bob Swafford. Reminded me that he was a doctor also. Dentists are sometimes funny that way."

We parted company, John giving Mary Ellen a peck on the cheek and promising to email me about the next night.

Mary Ellen and I found Velma asleep under the covers and apparently dreaming about something exciting, as her legs were moving as if she were running. I didn't need to rouse her. The answer to my question was displayed on her nightstand: two of John's cookies, one partially eaten, rested on a napkin.

I explained the gist of my working hypothesis to Mary Ellen as we made our way out. She actually gave me credit for clever thinking, though I'm sure she thought there still might be a screw or two loose. Still, with an email from John saying Robin and he would be happy to join us tomorrow night, we were following my favorite detective tool to a T: get involved parties together and see what happens.

Sean Carpenter is another doctor friend, a professor of psychiatry at Yale New Haven who makes biannual appearances, Christmas and Easter, at church. Sean would be a perfect addition to the steak fest, I thought. A few texts back and forth, and Sean and Betsy were confirmed.

Sean and I have played golf most summer Wednesday afternoons for years. We love it when we're matched with a twosome who don't know us. Sean likes to gamble, and puts some good-sized bets on the two of us against anybody. He's not a psychiatrist for nothing: inevitably, not much later than the second hole, one of the other golfers will ask, "So what do you guys do for a living?"

Then will come the fun. "Oh," I'll say, "Sean's a psychiatrist." That always leads to a step back and a raised eyebrow. "And what do you do?" the patsy asks me. "I'm a minister," I'd answer.

The other golfers always act nonchalant, like they play with psychiatrists and members of the clergy every day. But, in fact, they're plenty chalant. Suddenly, they need to think twice about their behavior lest their feared mental instability become obvious. Not least, they feel they can't cuss even when cussing is the only natural thing to do. From that hole on, we have them.

No sooner had we greeted Robin and John the next evening when Robin pulled me aside, Mary Ellen and John joining Sean and Betsy on the patio. "Richard, I'm really worried about John. He has this weird cough. If I didn't know better, I'd swear it was kennel cough. And did you see his new hair? He finally ditched his beret, but did you see his hair? He's been bald since I've known him, and now he has these thick, curly splotches all over. When I ask about it, he clams up. And he's always sniffing people. I've encouraged him to see one of his colleagues, but he laughs it off. Or rather snorts it off."

"Robin, I think I know what's going on. Or at least enough to be able to tell you there's good news and bad news. The good news is I'm positive he isn't having an affair."

"Thank goodness," she said, leaning back on the wall. "What a relief! But what's the bad news?"

I was about to explain my theory when I heard Stay barking and loud voices from the patio. "Stay, get down and stop sticking your nose in those places!" Mary Ellen was shouting.

Robin and I ran outside to see what was going on. Stay's target was none other than John, who was now cornered. I could tell from Stay's demeanor that she was at play, but John couldn't. I grabbed Stay's collar and pulled her away.

195

"Your dog is mad," John barked. But rather than step away, John advanced on Stay, getting down on all fours. It appeared that John was attempting to do to Stay what Stay had just done to John.

"John Grogan!" Robin shouted. "Sweetheart, what are you doing? Honey, please stop it!"

Sean had seen enough and dashed off the patio to his car. Robin was still pleading with John to get off his hands and knees when Sean returned with a syringe. I wasn't surprised, really. I knew Sean always carried his little black bag, a gift from his country doctor father on Sean's graduation from medical school. John's posterior made an inviting bull's-eye, and his thin cotton shorts proved no obstacle for the needle. Sean then dropped to his knees and cradled John while whatever it was he shot him with kicked in.

***

"Thank God Sean was there," Robin said outside John's hospital room three days later. We were standing with John's two brothers, who'd flown in from out west somewhere, and Sean, who had just arrived from his morning rounds. "And most of it makes sense," Robin went on, "the phone calls, texts, his long hours at Oak Lawn, even the beret. And I get it that the Canadian vet mixed a drug for pets into his cookie mix, but how did John find him in the first place?"

"He's a long lost cousin is what I heard John telling the police," I said. "As you know, John's a voracious reader, and he'd learned about a drug used by veterinarians in Canada to treat hair loss in dogs. John believed it would work in humans, as well. The drug isn't approved in the US, so John worked out an arrangement with his Canadian relative. Although it's technically illegal to ship drugs from Canada to America, authorities overlook small amounts, if they even check for them – they're after the big guys. In any case, there's no law about shipping baked goods like cookies. So, a little mixing of the tasteless drug into cookies, and, voila, it's a prescription by any other name. That the vet loves to bake cookies was a bonus."

"Robin, you've probably already figured out that John's days of practicing medicine are over," Sean said. "I understand he's had some harebrained ideas in the past, pun intended, but he really went too far with this. The state will confiscate his license without a hearing, given the publicity all this has engendered. But I do have a happy piece of news for you: Yale's Department of Dermatology is intrigued by the drug and is thinking about trying to fast-track it for FDA approval in humans. I was talking with the department chair no more than an hour ago, and he said he could find a place for John on his staff as long as he didn't treat patients. He recognizes John's genius and thinks he can keep him in check. So that's good, don't you think?"

"Of course!" Robin said. "But what about the patients in Oak Lawn who ate John's cookies? Are they going to be okay? Do you think they will sue?"

"I talked with the head nurse," I said, "and I think the only thing that might cause them to bring litigation is if they have to give back their hair. They don't even seem to care that it's thick and dog-like. I guess if you're bald, you're happy to have any kind of hair, shaggy or otherwise. And if humans react the same as dogs in Canada, they won't need any more of the drug. Once it kicks in, it's like turning on the hair machine forever."

"But what about the bizarre, canine behavior?" Robin asked. "I saw John scratching his ear all the way here in the ambulance."

"Yeah," one of the brothers said, "he was doing that when we walked in. Then he sat up in bed and held out his hand, like a paw."

"The side effects will go away once the medicine is stopped, I understand," I said. "Already has in most of the patients in the nursing home. Except for Velma the pee-er. But it turns out she's been a bit incontinent for several years, so the cookies can't be blamed for everything. But no one's happier with her hair than Velma. She's finally the blonde she always wanted to be."

"So all's well that ends well, I suppose," Robin said. "Richard, I can't thank you enough for solving this crazy affair. I'm so relieved. And Sean, you're the best. I think John will enjoy being a researcher. How can I ever thank you for all you've done?"

"Robin, you don't owe me anything," Sean replied. Then, turning to John's brothers, he asked, "Say, you guys wouldn't be free for some golf this afternoon, would you?"

The End

Ghosts

"Just yesterday, right during the service, the casket opened, and the body sat up." Charles Hampton was maybe six inches in front of me, his red-faced passion drawing attention from those in line behind him who must have doubted they were hearing what they heard. "I would've fainted," he continued, "but the shrieks were so loud I was distracted. Can you help me figure out what's going on?"

I badly wanted Charles to continue his story, but there were others waiting to greet me – the vacation-fill-in preacher – following Sunday worship at the Hillsdale Community Church. "Charles, can you go wait in the office? I'll be there as soon as I can," I said, pointing down the hallway. Charles Hampton, Jr is the owner of the Hampton and Sons Funeral Home, Hillsdale's oldest mortuary. Charles is not given even a little to levity, so I knew his comments weren't a prelude to a funny story.

Charles and I go way back – I'd pastored the Hillsdale Community Church for 30 years before retiring about a year ago. His roots, though, are much deeper in the town, he now being the third generation. A fourth is in the wings – 13-year-old Charles IV, called Gus. As all the Hamptons before them, they presently live in the apartment on the second floor of the funeral home. This might strike you as an odd thing to do. But it's a fairly common practice in the business – apparently, nothing says "we're here for you" like a funeral director living on site keeping watch over…whatever.

Curious to the max what Charles could have been talking about, I did my best "preacher hurry maneuver," grabbing hands and pulling parishioners past me. After all, it wasn't as if I'd returned to the pulpit after months of not seeing these people. In fact, since retiring and beginning my private investigator career, I'd been in the congregation most Sundays. Still, folks wanted to comment on my sermon, or tell me their opinion about my successor, Barry Roeder, or how the church was going to hell in a handbasket because of one reason or another, with tasteless organic, fair trade coffee during the Fellowship Hour being the latest tool of the Devil.

I found Charles in the pastor's study pacing back and forth and smoking up a storm on another of his Camel unfiltereds. "Charles, what are you doing? You can't smoke in here!" I shouted, tossing my black robe over a chair, peering up at the smoke alarm in the hope the battery was dead. "What's the matter with you?"

"Screw that, Richard," he said. "I'm going to lose my business, and you're worried about fresh air. For your information, the casket-opening, body-sitting-up act was but the latest bizarre episode. Earlier in the week, the wheels came off the gurney transporting a casket to the gravesite from the hearse. If one of the men hadn't caught it, the thing might have gone into the ground headfirst. Then yesterday, somebody hacked into our speaker system and played heavy metal music while the preacher was giving the eulogy. Everybody thought he was making fun of the deceased, who was well known to hate any music other than the kind Lawrence Welk played. That was Rev. Dunnam – the preacher, I mean. He said he'd never do another funeral with my establishment. Please, Richard, you're a private eye now. I beg you – help me!"

I said I would. I mean, this was fascinating – even *I* couldn't wait to find out who'd done it. The main concern I had was time. I'd agreed to cover for Barry during July while he and his family vacationed on Cape Cod. I didn't have to do all that much, really. Preach on Sundays, visit the hospitals, and stand by for – you guessed it – funerals. In the early days of my ministry, I might also expect a plea from a mother saying her daughter had to get hitched in a hurry and would I officiate. I don't remember the last time I received one of those appeals – thankfully.

I agreed to meet Charles that evening, my afternoon pledged to a movie with my wife Mary Ellen before being treated to one of our daughter Lucy's gourmet dinners. Lucy's meal was, as always, fantastic. I'm really a "gourmand," meaning I like to eat. So, most gourmet attempts are lost on me, but Lucy always inserts something – most likely butter – that leaves me wanting to lick the plate. Lucy's artistry in the kitchen is a recent discovery, her primary gift being floral decorating, a skill that also pays the bills for her store, aptly named Lucy's Flowers and Gifts.

"Dickie, tell Lucy about your new case," Mary Ellen said after Lucy returned to the table bearing a coconut custard pie, my favorite.

"The matter is hardly a secret with gossip being what it is," I began. "Seems the Hampton Funeral Home has had some strange goings-on, as in ghost visits, or more likely somebody is royally pissed off at Charles. Or I suppose it could be a prankster with a twisted bent having way more fun than he or she should. Thing is, he could be out of business soon if this keeps up. And what a shame. He's a bit high-strung, smokes like a fiend, but cares about serving the public in a classy way. I've known Charles for all my 30 years in Hillsdale. He'd recently graduated from embalming school and was working for his dad when I was hired by the church. We've probably done a couple hundred funerals together – maybe more. Can't imagine who would want to cause him such grief."

Following dinner, Mary Ellen went with me to the funeral home, where parking was tight, there being a viewing – or "wake" if you prefer – in progress, the funeral scheduled for the next day. The Hamptons' teenaged son, Gus, was waiting and guided us up the staircase to the family's living area. Charles and Clarissa offered coffee. I don't remember having eaten or drunk in a funeral home before, which may be the reason why the coffee had a formaldehyde note to it.

"First question," I said, placing my cup down with no intention of finishing the beverage, "is who are your enemies? Who would profit from seeing you go out of business?"

"That's just it, Richard. I've thought about little else in the last couple of days. And I can't come up with a soul. Not even the new funeral home in town, what does he call it, the Ellison Family Center. Sounds like a gym, but anyway, Burt Ellison would never do anything like this. He's a Mormon, very religious. He runs the funeral home over in Westford, too. We've hung out at conventions. But in any case, I can't see him involved, though he will certainly benefit." Charles paused and reached into his pocket and came out with a piece of gum. "Can't smoke in the house, drifts downstairs. This damn nicotine gum helps a little, at least until I can go outside and fill my lungs with the good stuff."

Clarissa filled the silence. "As you know, we hire several men part-time to help with the funerals, carrying the caskets, directing the parking and whatnot. Most of them are retired, have been with us for years. Never had a single cross word with any. There's the cleaning service, but they come when we're not busy, and sometimes weeks go by without us bumping into each other at all. I'm the only other employee, so to speak. Of course, Gus helps out here and there when he's not in school or involved in sports. That's it."

"So if it's not the competition," Mary Ellen wondered aloud, "if it's not any of your employees, who can it be?"

"That's why we hired you," Charles said, despair etched in his face. And then a woman screamed.

We dashed down the stairs to the viewing room and were met by Gus running up to fetch us. "Mrs. Murphy says she saw her husband's hand move," Gus said.

By the time we entered the room, hysteria had spread. "I saw Robert move his hand," the apparent Mrs. Murphy said. "He did. I swear. Look, don't you think it's closer to his waist than before?"

Mary Ellen and I had no opinion about the matter, but Charles and Clarissa and Gus peered into the handsome casket still yielding its fragrant cherrywood aroma. "Mrs. Murphy," Charles said, "Robert's hands are exactly where they've always been. I can attest to that. We measure all of our loved ones' hands from the center of their chest. I assure you, this is how we left him. And, besides, really! Your grief has you seeing things. You should talk with Rev. Burgess here. I'm sure he can help you."

"I know what I saw, Mr. Hampton. I have to leave now."

The four of us and Gus tried to calm the dozen mourners who'd been in the room, but they followed Mrs. Murphy to the door. "Mr. Hampton," Mrs. Murphy said, pausing at the entrance, "It's just like they're saying – you've got ghosts!"

***

I called Burt Ellison of the newly opened Ellison Family Center. Said I wanted to pre-plan my funeral. He was happy to see me at 2 o'clock. To my knowledge, I'd never met Burt Ellison. Still, because I may have had occasion to work with him in Westford, perhaps doing a funeral for a church member's parent, I decided I'd go incognito – I chose my blond wig and a similarly hued straggly beard. After years of dressing conservatively as a parson, trying not to stand out, I was really enjoying all my outlandish disguises.

For starters, the Ellison Family Center wasn't like any funeral home I'd visited. From woodwork to flooring to textured wallpaper that begged to be touched, everything was new, exploding with freshness, this in contrast to the usual stink of flowers, moldy carpets, air freshener plus whatever odor it was that made you think of death.

"Call me Burt." A man greeted me within two steps of my entrance, grabbing one hand with one of his while the other found my back, making for a half man-hug. This was definitely not my father's or anybody's father's funeral home.

"I have a traditional business in Westford," Burt said in response to my "wow!", "but Hillsdale is a progressive town, what with its proximity to Yale and all. So, I wanted to liven it up, if you'll pardon my pun, give it pizzazz, try to offer what nobody else does, especially the other funeral home in town, Hampton's. Not that there's anything wrong with what he does, just that, well, you know, it's the same old, same old. So far, people seem to appreciate our uniqueness. Come on in, have a seat."

Call-me-Burt led me to his office, pulled out a deep-cushioned brown leather chair and gestured to place my fanny therein. Stepping around the side of his ginormous desk, he said, "So, how did you hear about our little place here? TV, billboard, Yelp, a satisfied customer?"

"Read it about it somewhere," I said, not having given thought to the matter. "Sounded almost like fun."

"That's a good description of what we try to do at Ellison's," Burt said. "Funerals ought to be as fun as possible." For example, we have a theater room with a giant-screen TV and hostess service for nachos and drinks, soft drinks of course, me being Mormon. Stay in there if you want during the funeral – we don't care. The drive-through viewing isn't a novel addition to offer nowadays, but I already have next Saturday afternoon booked. The people don't even have to get dressed up. Drive in, look through the glass, push a button to record their names and drive away. Ten seconds max. Push another button, swipe a credit card, and they can have a spray of flowers sent to the grieving whoever. I mean, we have it all at the Ellison Family Center. Now how can we help you have the funeral of your life?"

Honestly, Burt had me at "snack bar." As if reading my mind, he said, "Where are my manners? Mr. Allen, come with me, we can have our discussion about how the Ellison Family Center can best serve you over some snacks in our Ellison Food Court."

Burt led me to a booth in the corner, bid me slide in, and returned moments later with my order of hot nachos, extra cheese, and a caffeine-free Diet Coke. He chose a Poland Spring water for himself. "I'm interested in what you offer that, say, the Hampton Funeral Home doesn't," I said, "and the cost for the various parts, casket, limousine, use of the space, etc. I assume all the extras you've told me about come with a price, right?"

Burt answered my question by saying their pricing was similar, the only difference being he hoped to make up in volume his higher costs. He continued, "Assume you've heard about the troubles Charles is having, the ghosts and all. Course I don't believe in ghosts, but the man has a boatload of problems. I've already had two people jerk their spouse out of there at the last minute. I mean, I'm glad to help, but I'll have to hire extra if this keeps up."

We continued a genial banter, but I'd heard enough – Burt was doing quite well enough without risking everything by sabotaging Charles. When the conversation slowed, I asked for a brochure with price quotes, and stood to leave. Burt returned with the same as well as a nice tote bag that included a coupon for a carwash in it.

***

I was helping Mary Ellen prepare dinner, my job being to place napkins, silverware and steal the occasional salad ingredient, when she turned on the 5 o'clock news. There, in front of the Hampton and Sons Funeral Home, a man about my age in a wrinkled suit a couple of sizes too large for him was speaking.

"Despite what you've heard, my client's reputation is at stake. There are no ghosts at the Hampton and Sons Funeral Home. We assure you that the Hampton and Sons Funeral Home has always been and continues to be a safe place for you and your family. We've retained a private investigator to investigate the investigation."

With a thank you of sorts, the camera returned to focus on the station's field reporter, who summarized the events of the last couple of weeks. She concluded, "There you have it. We're very live at the Hampton and Sons Funeral Home, where Halloween is making an early summer visit."

Since I was the investigator being hired to investigate the investigation, the pressure was now officially on to come up with answers, and the sooner the better. With Burt Ellison no longer a ghostly suspect, I returned to a detail that had been bugging me from the first conversation with Charles. After dinner, I reached the Hampton and Sons' answering service on the third ring and received a promise for a call back. Which happened as soon as I'd punched off my cell.

"Screening calls, can you imagine a business that screens calls?" Charles began. "Been receiving crank ones ever since the news was on. Last man wanted to rent the building for a vampire party. One before howled like a wolf. Richard, what am I going to do? A funeral home lives or dies with peoples' trust."

"Charles, I've ruled out Burt Ellison. Like you said, he doesn't seem the type to pull off something as mean as this. But I have a question. Remember how you told me a casket lid opened and the deceased sat up?"

"That's exactly what happened," Charles said.

"Surely you looked into it. I mean, somebody must have rigged it somehow. What–"

"Of course I checked it out. They'd connected invisible wire to the casket top and to the mattress. Somebody pulled on it from behind the curtain. Didn't see the wire at first; it's the kind we use for cosmetic purposes. You didn't think I thought it was a ghost, did you?"

"No, no. Just wondered what you'd turned up. Did you question all your staff about this?"

"Was the first thing I did. I can read people really well, tell you the truth. And I can assure you that everybody was every bit as horrified as my family and me. No way any of them would be involved."

"Would you be okay if I came over during a service, undercover of course, and snooped around? Though maybe first you should walk me through the building, back rooms and all."

"Sure thing. Only two funerals are booked – one tomorrow and one Thursday. The one tomorrow is at 10. Lillian Varney. Hardly any family. The Presbyterian guy from over at Westminster is officiating, Rev. Fuller. He's so short, he can't see over the lectern. So I pull up a side table, and he uses that for his notes. But you two must be acquainted. What're you going to say when you meet?"

"I think I'd rather not be recognized. I have a disguise in mind. Bet you won't even know me."

And he didn't. "Ma'am, Mrs. Varney's service isn't for another hour, but you may wait in here. And what fetching perfume you're wearing."

"Charles, it's me. Richard."

"Goodness gracious, Richard! I wouldn't have known you in the kitchen of your own home. That's quite a get-up. If Clarissa sees you, she'll be envious. But your voice needs some work."

I'd been in funeral homes almost weekly for 30 years, but apart from helping families choose a casket from the showroom, I hadn't been interested in checking out other behind-the-scene locations. Especially the embalming suite. I'll spare you many of the details since you've seen much the same on television or in movies, I'm sure: There were three stainless steel beds (I'll call them beds since it sounds better than platters). And bunches of tubes connected to bunches of bottles of liquid and bunches of drains. And bunches of power machines. And there was a smell the source of which I'm sure rhymed with "dehyde."

"Here's the media room," Charles said, gesturing to an alcove filled with electronic equipment. "Nowadays, we not only can pipe in any song but project photos and videos from the life of the deceased – about anything you can do on a computer. I understand some genius in some funeral home think tank is working on holograms, projecting the deceased into the room as he or she used to be, singing a song, dancing a dance, or swinging a golf club. Now *that's* ghostly to me, frankly. Anyway, you've seen the whole place. Any new thoughts?"

"No," I said. "None whatsoever."

I sat by myself at the rear of the chapel for Mrs. Varney's funeral. While a guest told a story about the dearly departed, I slipped out to see if there were any hijinks afoot. In fact, the rest of the funeral home was deader than a doornail. I knocked on Charles' office door. "Charles, so far we're cool. I'll hang around a while, but it appears today was the ghosts' day off."

I stood in the hallway outside the chapel with a view in all directions, but quickly grew bored. Mercifully, my phone dinged a text from the church secretary – "ring me."

Seated in my Subaru Outback, door wide open to release the sun's accumulated heat, I called the church. Shirley was in her late 70s, an employee I'd inherited when I arrived and who I vowed to replace as soon as possible. Why? In a word, she was insubordinate. Like she ran the church. Okay, so she did, but in time I learned this was a good thing.

"What's happening, Shirley?" I said when she picked up.

"Richard, I know you're not expecting to do any counseling, but Andrea Drucker phoned asking for you to talk to her son, Ben. Seems he got himself in some sort of trouble with the police. What shall I say?"

"Give me her number. I'll call her, see what's going on."

I'd confirmed Ben two years ago – nice boy, nice family. Andrea invited me to come over, said Ben was grounded and would be waiting for me. Said she wanted to put the fear of God in him so he'd never do anything like it again. Apparently, I was the fear of God's representative. I remembered Ben from the confirmation class as a freckle-faced kid who always did his homework, raised his hand a lot, and laughed at my jokes. In other words, he was the teacher's pet.

Andrea handed me a glass of iced tea and led me to the screened-in porch where a sad-looking tenth-grader-to-be stood slowly to greet me. "Ben, what's the deal?" I said, pulling up a porch chair to face him. "I reckon you have a good explanation for getting involved with the police. Right?"

The gregarious, polite to a fault, always smiling kid named Ben wasn't answering. I sipped my tea, allowing the silence to work the wonders that keeping my mouth shut usually does. And it did. "I didn't mean to hurt anybody, not really," he said.

"So what did you do?"

"Ordered a bunch of pizzas from Tom's," he said, barely audible. "On their website. Said I wanted 20 pepperonis. Just to see what would happen."

I bit. "So, what happened?"

"The owner, Tom, traced the online order to my computer. How was I supposed to know his brother was the chief of police?"

That filial relationship was no surprise to me, Chief Bob Blaney being as helpful as a lazy police chief could be in aiding me in securing my temporary PI license. "So what now?" I asked.

"I have to pay for the pizzas. Then, I have to write an essay about how stupid it was, which, I mean, is really stupid itself. I'd rather just write 'I was stupid' a thousand times. Then my folks have grounded me for a month – that's the worst part."

"Why did you pull a stunt like this? I know summers can be long and boring, but where'd you come up with this idea?"

Ben shrugged. "I don't know."

"Something tells me you're not alone in this."

"My folks and the police don't know this part. You won't tell, right? I mean, you always said you were a keeper of many secrets. So, okay, I was trying to get into the Dragon Cave Club. They make you come up with Dragon Deeds of Daring. Then, if they approve, you have to pull it off. You earn 50 points for each Dragon Deed, 200 if it makes the paper or TV. Get to 500 and you're in. Don't tell Mom or Dad, though, okay?"

Technically, privileged pastor-parishioner conversation in a parent/child situation is full of shades of gray. "For now. But that's all I'm promising. But one more question – did you have anything to do with the strange events at the Hampton Funeral Home?"

"No!" he said, too quickly in my estimation.I aimed to lower the tension on the porch by changing subjects to the Red Sox, Ben's and most Hillsdale kids' favorite team. We bantered a while, and I left him checking his phone for new messages. Andrea was busying herself in her office.

"Andrea, he's a mighty sorry young man. I don't think you need to worry much about him. Nothing but a prank – I could tell you some of my own. From long ago, I mean. He's just trying out new behaviors. And, besides," I added with a chuckle, "Tom was paid for 20 pizzas, so he's a happy camper."

Andrea didn't catch on to my attempt to lighten the situation with a dash of humor but thanked me for coming, and I left. As often was the case in my pastor days, I'd been helped more than I'd helped – I now was fairly certain who the ghost was at the Hampton Funeral Home.

My cell had vibrated in my pocket while on the porch. In the Druckers' driveway, I listened to the recorded message from Charles Hampton: "Richard, you'll never guess what happened at the cemetery. Rev. Fuller had a sneezing fit. Like nothing you've ever seen. Must have gone on for five minutes, I kid you not, one right after the other. Thing was, somebody had filled his prayer book with red pepper or some such. As soon as he opened it to begin the service, he was a goner. We finally hustled him out of there. It was awful."

"Who went with you to the cemetery?" I asked.

"Regular crew, Dave drove the hearse, Ernie drove the preacher in the limousine. Gus went with one or the other. The three friends or family drove their own cars. It was a small gathering as you saw at the funeral home. No strangers, if that's what you're getting at."

"You have another funeral for Thursday, right?" I asked.

"Yes, Amy Peterson's great uncle from up in Vermont. Left her husband and her a ton of money so they want to do him up right. No other family."

With a rush of ideas competing for attention, I said, "I have an idea, Charles. I'll need a master key. Also, the password to your security system. Also, I'm not going to tell you what I'm up to – you'll have to trust me."

"You're about the only one I can trust, Richard. But not even a hint?"

"Not even a hint," I said.

***

My great plan for Thursday's funeral included Mary Ellen, but she begged off, something to do with her being needed at the church thrift shop. "So, you're going to hide behind the drapery?" she said. "I don't think any of your fictional detective heroes would approve. What if somebody sees your shoes sticking out?"

"I'm betting Gus needs at least one more easy Dragon Deed of Daring to claim his membership," I said. "The funeral home is full of hiding spots, corridors, little rooms, draperies, curtains everywhere to soften the ambience. I could simply tell Charles my theory, but what if I'm wrong? Don't want that. Better to catch Gus in the act."

Thursday morning dawned hot and humid as do about all July days in Connecticut. Charles had left a master key for me underneath the large outdoor ashtray stand. I let myself in around 7 AM and quieted the beeping on the security alarm. Mary Ellen had a point about the simplicity of my plot, but I'm new in this business. And, besides, no self-respecting real detective in a novel would take on such an unspectacular, non-murder case as this, so give me a break.

I found two beautiful red oak caskets with velvet linings and satin pillows on stainless steel folding gurneys in the embalming room, including one with Amy Peterson's uncle in it. The chapel was accessed from there through a door with a small window covered on the chapel side by – you guessed it – a large floor-to-ceiling beige drapery puddling at the bottom. Should the sound system act up, I'd be able to pop over there with little trouble. The drapery featured a floral pattern, the flower images created by contrasting thicknesses of material, the thin portions sufficient for my peeking. Could hardly have designed it better myself.

I hastily surveyed the other rooms on the floor and found no surprises. Not wanting to stand for a couple of hours behind a drapery, I pulled up a chair near Amy's uncle, and opened the *New York Times* on my iPhone. Figured I had at least an hour before I needed to find a hideaway. I was wrong.

First, I heard the PA system; "Testing, testing" said a man, who I presumed to be one of the part-time guys setting up the chapel.

Then, a second or two later came the creaking of the steps from the back stairway on the other side of the wall where I sat. I was trapped. I saw my only option. And, yes, I climbed in.

Not with Uncle Pete – the empty one. I pulled down the two parts of the top, one lower half, one upper as fast as I could, squirming to find a level of comfort. And took a deep breath. Then, footsteps. I heard Uncle Pete's casket lid secured. Then, movement – me!

I wasn't sure, but I suspected I'd been delivered to the chapel, what with the smell of flowers wafting into my container. At first, I couldn't figure out either the purpose of my little ride, nor who had been my driver. The latter was soon clarified with a boyish sneeze and cough – Gus it was. No doubt, he was learning the business by carrying out jobs of increasing responsibility with preparing the chapel for a service likely the latest on his list of "to-dos." I tried not to think too hard about why Gus had chosen to wheel me in rather than Uncle Pete since Uncle Pete's casket was wide open and mine wasn't. Because, as you've probably figured out, the only reason for this daring deed scenario would be to bury an empty casket, a little punishment from Dad later for an "honest" mistake well worth it. What a hoot that would be! Dragon Club Cave membership, here comes Gus!

Because Gus didn't open the casket to reveal the body – me – I assumed the service had been planned as a "closed casket," a common practice for brief ceremonies where the dearly departed had been previously viewed by family. This was both good and bad. Good in that my hiding place wouldn't be *discovered*; bad in that my hiding place *wouldn't* be discovered.

Oh, and one more thing: Before padding out of the room, Gus turned the two locks on the casket lid. I was sealed for eternity.

All caskets have seals, watertight, airtight, with the more expensive ones having the most secure. A push on the top of my satin-lined box confirmed the successful engagement of the locks. Given the costliness of oak caskets, I had no doubt my air supply had begun a terminal countdown. Too late, I thought of what I should have done – demand Gus let me out and make him confess to his parents. I would've hit myself upside the head at this tardy realization, but there wasn't enough room.

"Excuse me," I said, way too politely for one in the fix I was in. Then, louder, "Hello. Anybody there?" I wondered if Gus's making my home airtight and watertight also meant it was now soundproof, though why one would want such a feature in a casket defied me. I also concluded I should save my breath. I also had to pee.

I'm reckoning a few hours went by, maybe one or two, maybe 24 – a pitch black environment does something to one's internal clock. That I hadn't wet myself encouraged me to believe it was closer to one or two. I'd noticed the air inside seeming humid, noticed the need to breathe more deeply than usual. Noticed I was on the verge of being scared to death. Then, voices – it wasn't soundproof, after all. Must be a cheaper issue than I'd imagined.

"I told Mr. Hampton we'd changed our minds. We wanted an open casket." A woman, likely the soon-to-be-rich niece.

"No problem, whatsoever, miss. If you'll kindly step out of the chapel, we can open the casket." A man had spoken, one of the part-timers.

"You can do it in front of me, it's not like it's going to be a shock. We haven't seen him in years, but dead is dead and he was old, so what's the deal?" That was Amy.

"I'm sorry, miss, but I'd lose my job if I didn't follow our protocol. It'll just take a minute to open and fluff the pillow and the like. You can have a seat in the foyer."

Even while listening to the locks being reversed, I realized it wouldn't be wise to sit up and say, "What took you so long?" That would lead to at least one heart attack of an innocent employee. With the air already fresher, I decided to wait and see what developed.

"Guy looks natural as all get-out," the male voice said, my closed eyes prohibiting spot-on identification.

"Charles is really a master with the make-up," said another man. "Did you see that old woman last week? If she'd have walked in off the street, I'd have asked her for a date. He's a pro's pro, I'll tell you." With a helper on either side, I was lifted and plopped down, the pillow shoved farther under my head until I was ready for my debut as a dead man.

"My heavens! He's much younger than I'd pictured," Amy said. "Almost looks like he could sit up and take nourishment. They didn't comb his hair very well though. You'd think for what we're paying they'd take care of that. There. That's better. Funny looking nose, too. Not like anybody's in the family. Must have grown since we last saw him. Should've had a nose job, taken some off the end about right here. Or maybe here. Or here."

Couldn't help it – I sneezed.

"Jesus, Mary and Joseph!" Amy shouted. Screams threatened to blow the ceiling off the building. From my newly upright position, I caught sight of multiple backsides in high gear, no doubt a few threatening to discharge their holdings.

"Excuse me," I said loudly to the last to depart.

The two helpers came running. "Holy moly!" one said. "Call Charles."

"Can you help me out of here?" I asked. But the two men who made Casper the Friendly Ghost look like a cheap imitation were also heading for the hills.

"What's going...?" Gus began, having dashed into the chapel. "Rev. Burgess! How'd you get in there?"

***

For the second time in a week, I found myself defending a young man to his parents. Or trying to, the task challenging my best effort. The family of Uncle Pete had been corralled in the parking lot and convinced to return. The minister, a cousin, arrived, and after the correct dead person was put in place, led the service. Burial followed. So now here we were, seated in Charles' office. Gus had spilled all the beans, prompted occasionally by me armed with my knowledge of the Dragon Cave Club operation. I could tell Gus wanted to ask me how I knew so much, but he didn't.

"So Richard, how do you suggest we inform the public that all is well? Sure as heck can't say Gus was behind it."

"Truth properly spun is no sin, or at least only a small one," I said. "Why don't you ask your attorney to issue a statement that a prankster has been discovered, and that you hope to win back the public's trust, maybe offer a discount or whatever funeral homes do. I'm bound to have a funeral in the next week or two, and as you know, the Hillsdale Community Church always uses Hamptons'. I'll make sure they do, in any case. Then word will spread, and you'll be back in business. As I always say, all's well that ends well."

***

I called Shirley in the church office to see if I needed to stop by the hospital before returning home.

"No," she said, "too late. Ernie died. Family wants to do a funeral next Monday. That good with you?"

"Sure," I said. "Where?"

"They wanted to do it at Ellison's Family Center," she said.

"Oh, no," I came back.

"That's what I told them. Said we only worked with Hampton's. Their choice: take it or leave it."

"Good going," I said, "the Hampton's will be forever grateful."

"Well, isn't that special," she said in her mocking church lady voice. "Anyway, hurry back here, Richard. Need you to proofread the bulletin before I leave – have a dental appointment."

"Be right there, Shirl. Be right there."

The End

Eagle's House

I wasn't afraid of suffocating – the wind rushing past my face in the old car's trunk told me oxygen was the least of my problems. More likely, my too tightly bound, now numb feet and hands would fall off, and I'd bleed to death. I was aware that my eyes were shut, though I didn't know why. I opened them and remembered – my curly black wig was six inches away, mocking me. This private investigator gig had taken a wrong turn. Oh, how I longed for a good old-fashioned church fight.

The week in late June had begun with a surprise. Eagle, aka Arnold Bowman and my partner in solving the ESPN celebrity Guy O'Neal caper, had landed a position in the engineering department at UConn. Seems someone had left the school a ton of money to endow a chair for a Native American engineering professor. Eagle heard about it at the community college in Arizona where he taught, and an application and interview later he was hired. Typical Eagle, he said not a word to me until the phone call Monday morning.

"Richard! How're you doing, Kemosabe?"

"Eagle, my man. Whazzup?" Eagle truly was my man. Beyond helping me in my first case, he'd rescued me from a storage shed in the blazing Arizona desert when I was sure I was a goner. This was after I'd intervened to prevent his son Frankie's kidnapping. In any case, no Eagle, no me. He'd always be *the Man* in my life.

"We're neighbors," Eagle said. "Or, sort of. At least in the same state. Got a job at UConn. Begins this semester, in a couple of weeks. Let's do lunch. Is that how Yankee preppies talk?"

"Eagle, wow! I can't wait to tell Mary Ellen." I walked through the house searching for my beloved, although I was fairly certain she'd gone down to the church to help with the food pantry expansion. "So where will you live?"

"Great deal on a big house in Storrs. Fully furnished, rent for now, option to buy. Frankie loves it. Has a swimming pool. Huge deck in the back. Lots of pool parties and barbecues in your future, Richard."

So that's how my unforgettable week started.

***

Mary Ellen and I were set to make the hour drive to Storrs on Wednesday when her cell rang.

"That was Deb," she reported, stuffing her phone back in her jeans pocket. There's a reporter coming from the *Sun* to interview us about the food pantry. Said since I was the chair of the program, I absolutely had to be there. You go along to Eagle's. We'll have Frankie and him over one day soon."

Eagle and I met at Chippo's Mexican Restaurant near the campus, where we downed a sampler platter each. "For cooks who've probably never seen more than a dozen Mexicans in their lives, they did all right," Eagle said. As always happens, we drew more than our share of lingering glances, Eagle being the personification of a six-foot six granite block with appendages and long black hair. I'd like to think a few folks wondered who his handsome, somewhat older friend was, but this may not have happened.

I followed Eagle about five miles to his new home, a typical New England colonial on maybe an acre of land, woods on either side, no neighbors in sight. There was an older silver Buick in the driveway with a woman climbing out, wearing a North Face jacket and ski cap. Seeing us slow down to pull in, she jumped back in the car. We parked, one in front of the other, next to her in the driveway.

She reopened her door, leaving it ajar, and swept her long blonde hair out of her face. "My name's Kathy," she said in a voice that could only be described as movie-star sultry. "My husband and I live down the road. Heard someone was moving in, thought I'd welcome you." We shook hands, exchanged smiles. "You'll find it's quiet here, nobody will bother you. Anyway, I just wanted to see if you were around. Welcome to Storrs, Mr. Bowman."

"How'd you score this cool place?" I asked while we shucked our coats in the entryway after bidding Kathy goodbye.

"Online," Eagle said. "Agency named Acela finds housing for lazy people. They send you videos inside, outside, interview local merchants, school principals, stuff like that. Principal was a very nice man. Said they'd keep a close eye on Frankie. Was as good as being there. If you want it, you send first and last months' rent plus a deposit, and they FedEx the keys. Smooth as silk. Vern – guy I talked to – even told me the owner was willing to sell. Have a seat – I'll grab the beers."

"So, you didn't have to attend a closing or do anything up here?" I asked, Heineken in hand. I'd had a couple at the restaurant – this needed to be my last.

"No, just paperwork. Used the notary at the library. Sign of the times. How's the PI business?"

"Sorta slow, but I'm not exactly living in an exciting, bustling place. Got some publicity from a couple of cases. That helped keep me busy for a while. But nothing lately."

"You miss your church?"

Of all the people other than church folks, Eagle had the hardest time understanding how a minister could suddenly up and quit after 30 years in the pulpit and take on private eye work. To him, me being ordained was almost like him being Native American.

"I miss some of it. But I don't miss the church politics and living in the fish bowl." I'd told him at lunch why Mary Ellen couldn't come, the food pantry addition and all. "Mary Ellen hasn't missed a beat. And I still find my place in a pew most Sundays. It's working out fine. I like the new minister."

Around 2:30, Frankie burst through the door, threw down his books, saw me, and stopped dead in his tracks. "Uncle Richard!" We hugged, and his dad excused him to go rustle up an after-school snack.

"Kid loves you, you know," Eagle said. "You saved his bacon before I saved yours. Sort of a mutual admiration society we have going here. One reason I didn't think twice about moving to Connecticut. Frankie doesn't have family except for me. Now you're family. I told him to call you 'uncle.' That okay?"

"I'm honored," I replied, aware of a little catch in my voice. With promises for future meet-ups, we soon parted. I was anxious to get home and hear how Mary Ellen's interview with the paper went. Turned out there was TV coverage as well.

"You've been on television several times, but this was my first," she said. "It was so exciting. They turned on this bright light and shoved a microphone in my face. I didn't know they'd asked me a question, so I just stood there. They must have thought I was hard of hearing because they shouted, 'Mrs. Burgess, how many needy people do you expect to serve each week?' I think I smiled, I know I meant to, and then I said something like 'I have no idea.' Which was silly because I know the answer – one hundred – but I was so nervous. So then I blurted out, 'One hundred! We expect to provide food and staples for at least a hundred people a week, twice as many as before.' They thanked me and told me I could leave. I'm still glowing."

"We'll have to make a point of watching the local news tonight," I said, "maybe record it if I can remember how to do that."

My cell rang its church bell chime. Little did I know that the bell was tolling ominously for me.

"Richard." Eagle spoke calmly though I detected something was amiss. "Something's amiss. Couple showed up fifteen minutes after you left – nice people, but not happy people. Said my house is their house. Worse, they never put it on the market. Worse, I have to get out. Worse, called the Acela man. Number's disconnected. I'm at the police station, but they're short-handed. Say they're too busy with a string of convenience store holdups."

"Good grief, Eagle. What the heck's going on? What are you going to do?"

"Police say there's a reasonable Quality Inn nearby. Suppose we'll hole up there. Put other stuff in storage somewhere. Tried that Kathy woman's number, also. No surprise – it's not in service, either."

"I wondered how she knew your name when we were on the porch. There's something more than amiss going on here, Eagle." I copied down what little information he had about Acela and Vern – whose last name was Smith (of course it was). I added Kathy's bogus phone number for fun. If I'd have had a clump of cotton candy, I'd have had more to work with.

I filled Mary Ellen in on the bad news and retired to my office – really a desk with a chair and my laptop in a spare bedroom. Stay, the golden retriever I inherited from an unlucky lady in a lavender Lexus, curled up in the footwell, her head on my foot. She loves when I do detecting work at my desk because I keep a pot of coffee at the ready in the kitchen. While there, I always toss her a treat from the pantry.

Suspecting Eagle wouldn't have done an extensive web search, I Googled "Acela." How great it would have been to find an active website with layers of contact information. But there wasn't. Instead, I had to wade through countless pages of hits, most recent ones having to do with the high-speed train in the northeast corridor. Eventually, I found "Acela Real Estate Professionals – Choose your new home without leaving your chair." It promised "offices in six states." That had to be the firm Eagle worked with. But I learned nothing more – couldn't get anything on the page to open, including the bright red "Contact Us" button.

***

Thursday morning broke beautifully if, like Stay, you enjoy lots of snow. I have to shovel a good-sized area for her to do her business, and if I don't also shovel a path to the business area, she cops an attitude. Worn out, I watched the snowplows finish and decided, what the heck, let's go to Storrs. I thought about calling Eagle for some company but figured he'd be busy enough plotting his and Frankie's next move. Since Mary Ellen had plans to meet with the owner of our local grocery store about increasing donations to the food pantry, I decided to go alone. Like my inspiration Spenser of the private eye novels, I like to engage all my senses in the pursuit of bad guys including getting a feel for the lay of the land, sniffing around, eyeballing the joint, and all the other sensory clichés mystery writers use. Plus, there's always the requisite eating at a local greasy spoon – taste matters, too.

The main roads to Storrs were fine, Route 195 barely wet. For a small state, ten miles this way or that can sometimes make a huge difference in weather. Storrs has grown in recent years, but at heart it's still a New England town with about as many cows as people.

Property information is public knowledge, I told myself, attempting to bolster my courage before I entered the tax assessor's office.

"Yes," I said to the woman about my age, pencil stuck in her tightly curled coif of cheaply dyed red hair, "I'd like to see the card on 49 Simpson Forest Way."

I could tell she wanted to ask why. Probably most people offered a reason, I reckoned, but if I knew my law, I didn't have to. So I didn't. She hesitated a moment, tapped a few keys on her computer, reached back to a printer and handed me pages detailing the property history of 49 Simpson Forest Way. I thanked her and left.

I toted my sheaf across the street to Danny's Café. Danny's was that iconic place in every town where locals gather to chew over how the world's going to hell in a handbasket. My mere entrance brought looks of suspicion from the gathered older generation of wise men and women who no doubt figured me for some professor-type or maybe father of one of those liberal, commie students at UConn. Not wanting to take one of the few remaining booths and risk upsetting a regular, I chose a counter seat, a chrome-and-red-vinyl-covered spinner-stool right out of yesteryear. The sticky menu was propped up between plastic ketchup and mustard squeeze bottles.

"The Number One," I said to Mavis who'd inquired, "What'll you have, hon?"

"Where's that on the menu?" she asked.

"What?" I said. "Where's the Number One?"

"I asked you first," Mavis replied, twitching her nose, suggesting she'd already spent more time with me than she wanted.

"I want a burger, fries, and a Diet Coke," I said. "On this menu, here, it's got this little number one in red next to it. Comes with coleslaw, too."

"Most people just say 'One,'" she said. "No need to say, 'number' also. Confused me." And with that she hollered to the kitchen, "One, no fluff."

No fluff? Was that a dig at me? I'd have thought I was eminently fluff-worthy, but I'd definitely need to check my meal for absence of fluff.

Mavis deposited my Diet Coke with a splash sliding over the glass rim. I wiped up the bubbles, then drew a slurp from the straw I'd plunged into the dark carbonation. More fully aware of my surroundings, I discovered I'd parked myself next to the case of pastries for the day. I was impressed with the length of the line that had formed for cakes and pies to go. Hard not to study what I could order if I wasn't already cheating on my diet. That piece of pecan pie would work. Oh, that woman snatched it. That woman! That woman was Kathy, Eagle's make-believe neighbor with the make-believe phone number.

Paranoia, I'm sure, but I strongly suspected I was standing out in Danny's Café no less than if I'd been wearing a sign saying "I don't belong here." In any case, I didn't want Kathy's attention at this point in my investigation. Spinning my red seat to the left, I headed to the restroom alcove in the back, hoping to buy some time and help my heart return to sinus rhythm.

"All yours," said a portly guy a couple years older than me wearing a well-used T-shirt with a gun on the front. He held the door for me, I said thanks, entered, breathed deeply to calm myself only to discover Mr. Portly wasn't a flusher.

My re-entry into the dining area went unnoticed except for my new friend who flashed me a grin, suggesting he'd enjoyed my bathroom visit much more than I. Kathy had finished her transaction of the pecan pie and was heading out the door. After re-claiming my stool, Mavis clanked down my "One" and the check with a hastily drawn smiley face. Sure, try to make up to me now, will you. I removed the partially toasted top of the bun to explore where fluff might have gone. Couldn't spot anything missing, and, frankly, the Number One looked great, though I'm hardly a connoisseur of burgers. Just cook the darn thing any way but rare and I'm a happy camper. As for the fries? Only McDonald's does fries worth a hoot. Otherwise, need to drown them with Heinz's best.

After wiping my greasy fingers on a series of paper napkins from the dispenser, I learned that the records from the assessor's office didn't hold much promise. Wasn't sure what I was hunting for exactly, but I'd learned in my So You Want To Be A Private Investigator course to explore every angle. "The Devil's in the details," was the school motto. Eagle's almost-house was built forty years ago, and the present owners, Carl and Marjorie Farr, bought it in 2000 for $250,000. The pool and deck were recent additions – schematics and jargon filled the pages.

I tossed a ten on top of the smiley-face and left, I'm sure, to the silent cheers of most. I'd noticed a real estate office, the Stone Agency, across the street and wondered what they knew about Acela.

"Never heard of them," Greg Bartles, fiftyish, with stylishly trimmed gray hair said. "Where'd you say you know them from?"

"Online," I said. "They brokered a rental for a friend of mine. I'll show you their website on your computer."

Greg was happy to oblige, having no other business than working on his own lunch, if the pizza box on his desk was recent. Sure enough, Acela popped up as before.

"Nothing works on this page," he said. "It's all locked up, probably shut down. But just looking at their site I can tell you that this sort of ruse isn't new to our industry. Someone buys a web domain, pays someone to design the page, makes up some testimonials, and ensures that Google will find them from any number of related searches, and they're in business. You watch *60 Minutes*?"

I confessed I didn't.

"I think they had something like this on not long ago," Greg said. "Outfit identifies a home in an isolated area where they know the owner is gone for a long time, break in, take pictures, videos, change locks then find a sucker – that'd be your friend, sorry – charge a few thousand up front, send you the key and vanish to start over in another state before the law can catch them."

We'd been joined by a younger man, thirtyish, in jeans and one of those polo shirts with an alligator on it who I took to be Greg's coworker or partner in the business. "Parker Stone meet, uh, what'd you say your name was?" Greg asked.

"Jim," I lied. "Jim Burleson."

"Parker's family own the business. Have owned it for years. They let me work here because of my people skills. Say I can charm the bark off a tree. By the way, prosperous-looking man like you, why don't you let me show you a few properties for investment. Name your price. I can get you something and you'll make a fortune in no time."

I saw what he meant about charm – a millennial wouldn't want to be called "prosperous." Guy my age? You bet.

I thanked Greg for his time, waved at Parker who I caught copping a piece of Greg's pizza – I'm pretty sure he raised an eyebrow but otherwise remained mute – and stepped out into the early summer's warmth. Found myself driving through the Dunkin' Donuts for a couple of glazed sticks, a kind of compensation for the pecan pie I missed but hadn't forgotten. Thus armed, I aimed for home.

I was startled by a large white van in our driveway, satellite dish on top, "KETV-10 4 U" plastered on the side. I was a detective. I detected a TV truck. Why? Not a clue.

"That's my husband, Rev. Burgess," Mary Ellen exclaimed, as I shoved open the door between garage and house. A blinding light blinded me, though I made out a man with a microphone heading my way while a camera and its operator pivoted accordingly.

"What do you think about your wife being named 'Hunger Advocate of the Year' in New Haven County, Rev. Burgess?"

"I think it's well deserved," I said, having no idea what was going on.

Satisfied with my eloquence, the television people returned to fawn over Mary Ellen. I surmised that this had to do with her telling everyone from the governor on down that they would be supporting the food pantry's addition and renovation. Telling them that separation of church and state be damned, they'd work together for the common good. Even in retirement from teaching, Mary Ellen knows how to get people to do what they ought to have done in the first place.

***

Greg's earlier appraisal of Eagle's dilemma sparked a notion. If the modus operandi of such bad guys is to do the deed and beat it out of town only to set up another operation, then wouldn't it make sense I might find them via my partner in the business, Google Search?

Stay loved my thinking and once again warmed my feet with her ample blondeness.

By combining words such as *real estate, lazy* and *without leaving your chair,* I found my quarry in no time. Actually, several. One in Rhode Island, though, stood out: same red button for "Contact Us," but this one worked, leading me to a page with a "Chat Now?" feature. I tabbed "yes" and waited.

"Vern has entered the room. Please wait." If this was Vern Smith, I was going to hoot. But it wasn't: it was Vern Jones. I hooted anyway.

Mr. Jones wanted to know how he could help me. I gave him a spiel about needing to move to Rhode Island in a few months, but being a busy guy, blah, blah, blah. Wanted to rent, maybe buy later.

He bit. Said he had just the house for me, that he'd send me the video and we could go from there.

A download later, I was staring at a property outside of Providence, being given a full tour. Lovely music played, a sexy woman's voice commenting on each of the rooms of the lavishly furnished home. I saw no humans but had a strong hunch I was dealing with Vern and if I retained any voice memory, Eagle's almost-neighbor, Kathy.

No sooner had the credits finished rolling than I received an email from Vern. He invited me to call him first thing Friday morning so we could talk business.

***

"Whatcha think?" he asked. "Look like something you'd be interested in?"

"Well, sure," I said. "How much do they want for it, you know, monthly rent and stuff?"

"You're pretty isolated here," Vern said. "Neighbors few and far between. It's quite a desirable area. They want $2,500 a month. First and last and same amount for a damage waiver. Our firm adds 10 percent to the total. So, that'd be $8,250. I'll need a bank check along with some paperwork I'll get to you. Send it back, and I'll FedEx you the keys. Can have you in the house inside of a week. How does that sound?"

"A week?" I said. "I don't have to move that quickly. I was thinking more about a few months from now."

"Jim," he said, responding to the Jim Burleson alias that seemed to be working for me. "Jim, I'm not supposed to tell clients, but the owners are going to increase their asking this spring, taking advantage of the nicer weather and all. If you have any plans to move to Providence, you'll end up saving money by locking it in now. They're willing to do a two-year contract. And you said you might be interested in buying. Turns out, they'd love to sell. We could put all that in the contract so you'd be all set, no surprises."

"You know? I'm not all that far away. Why don't I pop down and take a run-through, say later this afternoon."

"Jim, no need to do that. Our job is to make your house hunting job easier. You've seen it all, nothing you haven't seen except the attic. And if that's important, I can video that to you."

In any other circumstance, I would have hung up – Vern was verging on pathetic in his pitch. I'd been scammed oodles of times as a minister with stories that would make Hollywood envious. Once a woman called me and other pastors in town a week before Christmas saying her mother had just died and she needed plane fare to go back to Chicago for the funeral. Did the same the next year. And the next. I finally asked her, "How many mothers do you have?" Fortunately, she only got one round trip out of me.

"Look, Vern is it?" I said. "This is a pretty serious commitment I'm about to make. I'm no more than a couple of hours away. How does 4 o'clock sound?"

Vern was quiet for a couple of beats. "Uh, my schedule's pretty tight. Okay, 4 o'clock. GPS should bring you right to the front door."

I called Eagle and filled him in. "Richard, you're something else. Sounds like Vern and Kathy to me, all right. Have never been to Rhode Island. I'd go with you, but Kathy would recognize me and things might go south."

I couldn't disagree. As I've mentioned, Eagle stands out. In fact, I'd bet not a single person who'd ever seen him has forgotten him.

"No problem," I said. "I'll wear a disguise because she'd likely make me also from our porch meeting."

"Richard, you know how you have a way of finding trouble, you and your preacher brain that thinks good intentions will save the day?"

I assumed he was going to finish his thought, but the silence on the line demanded a response. So I said, "Uh, yeah."

"Send me the address and text me every couple of hours or so."

"Eagle, that's mighty nice of you, but these people are money scammers, not violent criminals. Worst they do if I call their bluff is head for the hills. I'll give you a call tonight and tell you all about it."

***

Believe me, I never intended to own a closet full of disguises. But I did, owing to previous cases. A couple of wigs, woman's and man's, facial hair glue-ons, not to mention a woman's pant suit, earrings, brassiere, plus a make-up kit. Decisions, decisions. I chose my manly, curly toupee that cried out "wig here!" and added a soul patch. I looked weird, but so do a lot of people. If someone wants your money, they aren't going to care about your appearance – right?

My GPS performed as predicted, and Vern and Kathy appeared as soon as I'd opened the Subaru Outback's door. We shook hands, Kathy's right eye squinting a bit, but I couldn't read anything into it. I decided there on the spot to add to my camouflage with a "hard-to-get" gambit.

"Listen, before we check it out," I said, "I need to be honest with you. I can't do $2,500. $2,250 is tops. Maybe you can show me another property in my price range."

Not surprisingly, Vern said he was optimistic the owner would go for it. Kathy nodded her head vigorously in agreement. "I'll call them while Vern shows you around. Did you bring a check, Mr. Burleson?"

"Have it right here," I said, patting the billfold in my back pocket.

I won't bore you with the details of the tour except to say it was a nice house. Hard to tell about the pool as it was covered, but the professional landscaping around it suggested a top-flight installation. Place was worth every bit of the $2,500, if not more.

Kathy, reeking of cigarette smoke, joined us after slamming the back door, preserving a measure of cool in the unair-conditioned house. "So, what do you think, Mr. Burleson? Owners say they'll take the $2,250. We've got the simple contract right here. Nothing fancy. I'll just fill in the new amount and we're in business. Can give you one of our keys for starters. You're getting a great deal, Mr. Burleson."

I affected thoughtful consideration.

"You do have a check, right?" Kathy said.

"Sure, sure," I said, pulling my billfold out, feeling obliged to prove it, I guess. I say, "I guess," because no other reason for what I did makes any sense. One might also wonder what could possibly go wrong with such a gesture. One might even wonder what could go wrong after I fumbled my billfold and it landed *ker-slap* on the floor, veteran of a gajillion similar oops! But then one would cease to wonder when Kathy, a helpful woman, obviously, joined me in trying to pick up my splayed-open wallet. That is, our heads hit together, a real seeing-stars kind of banging. But nothing hurt as much as seeing my curly wig flip to the floor beside the cursed wallet.

"Oh, my goodness!" she said, stepping back as if unsure whether it was alive. Then, boring a hole through me with her eyes, she exclaimed, "I thought you looked familiar. You're Bowman's friend, aren't you!"

"Bowman's friend?" I tried. "Please excuse me. I'm so embarrassed. I should leave."

A hand squeezed my upper left arm until what muscle I had was surely turning to mush. Vern was obviously stronger than he appeared.

"What're we going to do, Vern?" Kathy asked. "We can't just let him leave. I told you we shouldn't have agreed to meet him."

My arm was first twisted behind me and bent upward before I was marched toward the front door. Outside, the trunk of their old silver Buick LeSabre was squeaked open, and I was lifted, then pushed inside, my coat and wig following.

After several stops, starts, turns – getting out of the driveway and neighborhood, I presumed – a smoother ride ensued. Semis passed us and we passed them – Interstate 95, undoubtedly. Which way – toward Boston or New Haven – I couldn't tell. Thing was, I wasn't afraid of suffocating – the wind rushing past my face in the old Buick's trunk told me oxygen was the least of my problems. More likely, my too tightly bound, now numb feet and hands would fall off, and I'd bleed to death. I was aware that my eyes were shut, though I didn't know why. I opened them and remembered – my curly black wig was six inches away, mocking me. This private investigator gig had taken a wrong turn. Oh, how I longed for a good old-fashioned church fight.

After maybe an hour we slowed and stopped. Near my head, the gas filler door opened and a rush of fuel began. Now that would have been fine – gas is fine. But I could smell it, and that wasn't so fine. Truth be told, it was horrific, like the trunk was being filled with Exxon's or Shell's cheapest. I tried to figure out why this was occurring, but even if I was the smartest person on earth, such wasn't going to keep me from becoming very sick – or worse. I hollered, "Help me!" I hollered, "Man in the trunk!"

"Shut up in there," Vern said, banging on the trunk. "I've got a gun, and believe me I'll use it."

I heard the typical noises of a gas purchase's conclusion, and felt the car rocking as Vern re-entered. I'd like to say the gas smell was abating, but it wasn't. Funny what you worry about in life-and-death circumstances: I was concerned that I'd puke on my black wig. Mary Ellen would have a fit – she'd make me throw it away. My fears of the future, however, were short-lived.

The car rocketed away but soon lurched to a stop, which is when the sirens I'd been unconsciously ignoring increased in decibels such that I thought my ears might burst. Men shouting, "Put your hands where we can see them! Step out of the car slowly! Walk backwards toward me!" I knew at that moment that I was going to write a hymn someday using those exact words.

The trunk lid was flung upward, and the first face I saw was Eagle's. Men in State Police uniforms bustled in the background, and I caught a glimpse of Kathy as she was led away.

"You're lucky that I don't think you have a brain," Eagle said, conviction rising in tandem with volume. "Followed you to the house, waited in a hot car. Could've rescued you there, but wanted to see where they might go. Luckily, State Police believed me."

"Well, thanks for letting me have a free ride. I almost died from the gas fumes, not to mention the claustrophobia. Hope it was all good for you!"

"The thanks I get. Why don't you crawl back in and I'll slam the lid down."

"No need to be sarcastic. Gas fumes are no fun. Thank you – okay? Darned glad you think I don't have a brain."

Eagle and I were the guests of the Connecticut State Police at the Westbrook, Connecticut, barracks. We told them the details, they patted us on the back, and we left, Eagle to Storrs, me to Hillsdale.

I called Mary Ellen on the way and filled her in. She didn't sound happy, even knowing I was safe. "Why did I hear about your escapade from reporters before hearing it from you?"

"Sorry, honey, but–"

"Don't 'sorry, honey' me, mister! You promised no danger in this work. You could've been killed, Dickie! You better never say a prayer without giving thanks for Eagle. That's all I got to say."

And that was all she had to say.

I drove the rest of the way in silence, lost in my thoughts, well aware of what might have been. But honestly? I'd never had such a terrific adrenaline rush in my life, toxic gas fumes excepted.

***

Stay welcomed me inside, but she was the only female in the house speaking to me, Mary Ellen having pulled the covers over her head. I grabbed a beer from the fridge and punched the TV remote. A familiar Westbrook barracks was in the background, a reporter and State

Police spokesperson detailing the events of my life over the past several hours. Footage from the perp walks of Kathy and Vern was inserted, and the male reporter who couldn't have been more than 14 years old concluded, "So there you have it. We have a new dynamic duo in our state and it's not Batman and Robin. No, it's Richard Burgess and a man they call Eagle. Criminals beware. Back to you, Erika."

The import of hearing myself referred to in the third person on the local news still hadn't fully registered when the phone rang.

"Mr. Burgess. This is KETV news calling. We'd like to set up an interview with you for tomorrow. We'd like to do it at your office – that be okay?"

I couldn't think of a good reason why not and a bunch why it was a great idea, as in more business for yours truly. The KETV man said they were also contacting Eagle, hoping he'd join us. I agreed to meet them at my little strip mall office around 10.

***

I brought Stay with me on Saturday morning over only a mild protest from Mary Ellen. What's better than a Dynamic Duo than a Dynamic Duo with a Wonder Dog? Stay, after all, had been the heroine in my last two cases, the unlucky lavender lady and the one starring my odd brother-in-law. I wasn't all that surprised to see Eagle pulling himself out of his Corvette as we drove into the lot – only the most secure people don't relish attention. I mean, look at the pope – is he having a ball up there on that balcony or what?

Eagle's presence didn't shock me, but the number of other TV trucks did. A podium had been dragged from somewhere and now occupied center stage on the sidewalk in front of my office door. Myron – my official mentor, supervisor, and office suite mate – had materialized and was shooting the breeze with a gorgeous too-much-hairspray redhead. Her darting eyes, wishing-she-could-be-anywhere-else kind of darting eyes, spotted Eagle and me and broke away from Myron, probably in his mid-sentence explanation of how he surveils the criminal class.

"Good morning, guys," she said. "We've got a huge turnout, television, local print media, even a dude from the *Boston Globe*. My boss wants us to stand behind that ugly lectern or whatever, says it'll look fine on TV. More official or something, I suppose. Anyway, because we broke the story, I get to ask a few questions first, then open the floor to others. Ready?"

Roxie, her name was. Roxie began, "Three, two, one. Good morning, ladies and gentlemen. I'm Roxie Reynolds of KETV-10 4 U News, and we're here this morning to interview Richard Burgess and Arnold Bowman, also known as Eagle. As you may know, the harrowing account of their pursuit of justice has gone viral." I sure as heck didn't know that; Eagle's face suggested he didn't know what she was talking about, either. He coughed, making me wonder if he thought there was a virus going around he should watch out for.

"Mr. Bowman – may I call you Eagle?"

"Eagle is good."

"Eagle, the State Police informed us of the details of the crime and the role you played in helping them catch the home scammers, but how did you know to follow Mr. Burgess?"

"Mr. Burgess isn't all that bright. Should have stayed a minister. But he wanted to help. I didn't think he'd turn up squat because, as I said, he's not all that bright at detective work. Thinks a wig is all he needs. What he needs is some street smarts. Anyway, I followed him because I knew he'd screw up somewhere."

Apparently, Eagle was still upset about my meager expression of thanks the night before.

"Mr. Burgess, you must be counting your lucky stars to have a friend like Eagle. Right?"

"Uh, sure," I said, strongly tempted to use Roxie as a medium to scratch back at Eagle. "Sure, Eagle's the man," is what I said instead.

"But, Mr. Burgess," she went on, "your detective ability was crucial in solving the mystery. You're obviously pretty good at what you do, street smarts or not."

Take that, Eagle old buddy!

The remainder of the 30-minute press conference included maybe three questions asked a dozen different ways, the exception being one posed by Roxie at the end: "So, what are you two going to do to celebrate?" Remembering the Copper Kettle Inn that we passed near Storrs, I offered it as a destination. Eagle raised an eyebrow and shrugged. "Would have to be Monday at noon. Rest of the week is complicated." That we'd chosen a televised news conference to discuss the details of our celebration would, in hindsight, be deemed an innocent blunder. *Blunder* as in *death wish*.

Unaware that this case was far from closed, Eagle and I were thanked by Roxie and received a few handclaps from the working press. A woman exiting the nail clinic next door paused, appraised the situation, and asked Eagle for his autograph. She gave me the up-and-down, shook her head, and left in quest of her car. I should also note that Stay received notoriety in the form of a picture of her that would appear on the front of most cities' newspapers the next morning. Seems one of the reporters had pulled out a muffin from her pocket. Stay lives for such easy prey.

***

Sunday was filled with phone calls for interviews following the TV stations' playing of the interview, not to mention the newspaper picture of Stay the muffin-snatcher. As it happened, I wound up talking to so many people that I never did get around to heading off to church. Mary Ellen said everyone asked about me, the preacher even naming me in his pastoral prayer. Miracles abound! I assumed Eagle was having a similar experience. Don't know about him, but I was having a great time with my newfound celebrity.

Our air conditioner broke Sunday night, of all nights, as the humidity and heat was on the way to record heights. Since having central air installed, we've become unusually intolerant of any conditions other than ideal. Easily spoiled, I know. Anyway, I had my hand on my cell to phone Eagle and cancel our lunch, but Mary Ellen said she'd call the service man if I'd take Stay for her morning constitutional.

"Nick, the owner of the company, said he'd come personally right away, considering how you put your life at risk for our country," Mary Ellen said. "Anything to help the Dynamic Duo, he told me."

"For the country!" I sputtered. "My Lord, all this is being blown out of proportion. Next thing, somebody will call with a great deal on a used Batmobile."

***

The Copper Kettle Inn sits on Storrs' highest hill overlooking the gorgeous, sprawling campus and the town's main drag. Traditionally the highest rated restaurant in *Connecticut Magazine*'s annual review, the Inn, as it's known, has a few pretensions, one being valet parking. You couldn't park your own car here if you wanted to. The valet will welcome you, park your car, return it to you when you are ready, and stick out his hand for at least a fiver. That wasn't actually written any place, but I'd heard about it from friends.

I paused at what had to be the valet's empty booth adjacent to the entrance, thinking for a moment that on the most miserable of days when I'd have paid a fortune for a valet, I'd have to do it myself. But, not to worry, here he came around the corner, wearing a Red Sox cap and one of those flimsy white air masks people use who want to avoid pollution. Didn't say a word, just held the car door for me, hopped in and zoomed away. Didn't even give me a claim check. Maybe the Inn's valets have to pass a facial recognition ability test of some sort – that would certainly qualify for another display of pretension.

Eagle had handled the reservations, and I'd forgotten to ask what name he'd put them under. Bowman didn't work. Neither did Eagle. I tried Arnold with no luck, either. At this point, I figured out another of the Inn's pretensions: maître d's who get a kick out of looking down their noses at people who don't measure up. I was out of bullets. I turned around and ran smack dab into Eagle.

"Yes, sir, may I help you? This gentleman was just leaving," Mr. Pretentious Ass said to Eagle.

"Reservations for two. Name's Burgess." Go figure.

We'd barely given our drink orders when I saw a man approach the maître d', whisper something to him, and watch while Mr. Officious Gatekeeper hustled away. The valet with a Red Sox cap and white mask to whom I'd given little thought appeared instantly familiar as he whipped off his disguise and searched the half-filled room. Parker headed our way.

"Parker, is that right?" I said, extending my hand. "What's with the valet gig?" You'll remember Parker as the lazy managing partner of the real estate agency, the one Greg worked for, Greg being the guy who put me on to the widespread scamming racket in the first place.

"I need you two to come with me," Parker said, gruffness and urgency coloring his words.

Eagle stood up, towering over the smaller man by a good eight inches. "And why should we do that?"

"Because I have a gun and you don't," Parker said, revealing a nasty looking snub-nosed issue in his coat pocket. "Some people you don't want to mess with don't approve of your recent activities. Let's go."

I could tell Eagle wanted to test his fisticuff skills against Parker's, but out of respect for my welfare, perhaps, he didn't. "Where are we going?" I asked, hoping he'd say some place cool. Parker ignored me.

I tried to signal our distress to our waiter with eye movements as we proceeded by the kitchen entryway, but he only smiled, thinking we were heading to the men's room or maybe that I was making a play for him. As we passed a storage closet near the front door, my old friend the maître d' and a man who appeared to be a manager-type were in full panic mode: "Call 911, he's unconscious!" Likely the honest-to-goodness valet had just been discovered. Taking our leave, Parker, Eagle, and I could have been stark naked and they wouldn't have noticed.

Our first destination was the white Cadillac Escalade parked maybe 50 feet away. Parker shoved us onto the generous rear seat and joined us, his gun no longer hidden. A man with a thick black beard slotted the gear selector into Drive, and drive we did.

***

As a minister's wife, I'd long since become used to Dickie being AWOL. Sometimes he'd call and check in; sometimes he'd forget. I understood – as long as he curled around me at night, which he always did, sooner or later. Since his retirement, however, he'd become more thoughtful, a steady diet of texts declaring his movements, even in his new PI thing. Which is why as late afternoon approached without a word, I sent him a text: "where r u?"

An hour later, I phoned him but heard only his "I'm on a case, will get back to you," recorded message. So, I'm sorry, but I began to worry because, one, Dickie never ignores my calls, ever. And, two, cell phone coverage in Connecticut is border to border. Something was up, and given his recent ride in a trunk, I imagined the worst.

I checked our family Gmail account for Eagle's contact information. Texts and phone calls to him weren't answered either. I remembered Dickie saying Eagle and Frankie were taking a room at the Storrs Quality Inn, so I found that number and called. I was put right through. Frankie picked up.

"Hi, Frankie. This is Mary Ellen Burgess, I'm Richard Burgess's wife. Richard and your dad were to have lunch today, and, well, I'm wondering if you know where they might be."

"No, Mrs. Burgess, I don't," Frankie said. "Tell the truth, I'm not sure what to do. Dad said we were going out for pizza tonight. Usually he's home by now. I tried to text him, but he hasn't got back to me."

"Right. I did the same with my husband. They were going to the Copper Kettle Inn, right?"

"That's what dad said."

I wasn't sure what to propose. I didn't want to upset Frankie, but it sounded like he was well on his way, regardless. "Let me make another phone call and I'll call you back," I said.

The Copper Kettle Inn person I spoke to reported confidently that "Burgess, party of two" checked in but left abruptly. That did it for me. I called Frankie.

"Frankie, I'll find the Quality Inn. Give me your room number. I'm sure there's nothing to worry about, but I'm going to feel better playing detective myself."

Before leaving, I called the Storrs Police to see what they could do. "Ma'am," the jaded voice on the other end began, "if we investigated every husband who hasn't been seen in 24 hours let alone five hours we'd never do anything else. Give it time. I'm sure they're off having fun somewhere. Keep checking your phone. Besides, we're out of manpower with the convenience store heists. You heard about them, right?"

On any other occasion, the idea of my husband "off having fun somewhere" might have been somewhat disquieting. On this occasion, I prayed it was true.

I opened the door to my Mini Cooper and Stay squeezed in, half in back, half in front. I had to push her aside to shift the gears. For whatever reason, Stay loves riding in my car.

Frankie was waiting for me out front, his concern probably having risen to the level of mine. Stay unhappily made herself comfortable in the rear, politely yielding a seat for Frankie, who directed me to the Copper Kettle Inn.

"I distinctly remember the gentlemen about whom you're inquiring," the maître d' said, his nose rising ever higher with each word. "I'd just come on. They had trouble with the name on the reservation until the smarter of the two, a giant man, remembered it. We had an unfortunate incident around that time, but I understand they left in a hurry. Perhaps their waiter could give you more information. In the meantime, madam, unless that's an official service dog, you'll have to take it outside. No pets allowed."

I assured the oh-so-caring man that Stay was my therapy dog saving me from violent outbursts of rage. He objected no further.

"Sure, I remember them," a waiter named Tony said. "How could I not? Ordered drinks, and shortly thereafter they left with Parker. The shorter, older one was giving me the come on. Stiffed me for the tab, too."

"Parker?" I said. "Who's Parker?"

"Real estate guy, family owns a real estate agency. A real jerk. One of those who woke up on third base and thought he'd hit a triple."

Stay had been acting funny, that is not doing her usual routine of sitting and panting and waiting for mama to do something, when all of a sudden she bolted back to the maître d's stand. From the back of it, she pulled Dickie's plaid golf cap and ran back to us, the maître d' in hot pursuit.

"I say, that dog has stolen a cap from lost and found. What kind of mutt is it? I must ask both of you to leave. Or shall I call the manager."

Ignoring the snooty man's outrage, Stay began a barking pattern I'd come to know well. That is, Stay was saying, "I smell Dickie. Dickie always has food. Let's go find Dickie."

I thanked Tony, stuffed a twenty into his hand for the unpaid bill, and the three of us departed, our car returned to us with a smile when I handed the valet a five.

Tony said the real estate agency was on Main Street, couldn't miss it. We entered, Stay loving Frankie's constant attention. "I need to speak with Parker," I said. "Is he in?"

"No, ma'am. I'm Greg. Can I help you? Hey, young man – cool cap, you've got there. Saw one just like it yesterday."

"Seriously?" I said. "Because I'm looking for my husband, who may have come in here yesterday. Richard Burgess is his name."

"No, don't recognize that name. Burleson or something, like the former Red Sox shortstop. Jim Burleson, I think it was. Love the cool cap, though."

Since Dickie's mother's maiden name was Burleson, I was certain I was on his trail. But that being many hours ago, the trail was fast growing colder.

"So could you give me Parker's number?" I said. "I was told to ask for him."

"Sorry, Parker only gives his number to his clients," Greg said. "You'd come fifteen minutes earlier, you'd have run into him. Dashed in and out, off to wherever Parker goes these days."

"Where's his office?" I asked.

"Oh, Parker doesn't have an office, uses that desk over there. Why?"

"Frankie, bring Stay," I said, leading both of them to Parker's desk.

"What are you doing?" Greg asked.

I didn't answer but yanked open a few doors until I found a pair of gloves.

"These will have to do," I said to Stay and Frankie. "Stay, take a whiff."

Since Stay smells everything anyway, sticking a couple of gloves in her face was a welcome invitation to fun. We'd never trained Stay to follow scents – I mean, why would we do that? – but something told me our Stay was gifted.

I rubbed Dickie's golf cap and the gloves together and offered the combination for Stay's examination. She got it – she was going to search for the man with the gloves because he was connected to her master, who always had food. Sometimes, you just have to think like a dog.

Frankie and I left a puzzled Greg as we followed Stay out the door and down the street, her nose a quarter inch off the ground, sweeping left to right. Stay stopped in front of Harry's Hookah Hangout, whimpering animatedly in her desire to go inside. We entered.

"Hey! No dogs in here," shouted a man who un-sucked his pipe and stood. "And no kids, either. What are you, lady, nuts?"

I might have asked the man if Parker was present in the den of smoke, but Stay took off and jumped up on a patron seated in the rear. "Are you Parker?" I asked, joining them.

"Who're you?" he came back.

"I asked you first," I said. "This young man and I are looking for his father and my husband. They were last seen with you. I want to know what you've done with them."

"Ma'am, you must be mistaken. I don't have the foggiest what you're talking about. You're confusing me for someone else. And to tell you the truth, I don't appreciate your accusations."

"Parker, you're not helping yourself," I said. "My dog has a nose for the truth, and you're coming up way short."

I stepped back, out of range of Parker's hearing and punched 911 on my cell's screen.

"What's your emergency?"

"I'm at Harry's Hookah Hangout, and there's a terrible fire. Come quickly." I hung up.

I'll say this for Storrs: their first responders respond in a hurry. In no time, sirens surrounded the building, fire and police personnel rushing the room. "Where's the fire?" they all inquired in unison.

A dozen or more sets of eyes of semi-stoned customers scanned up and down, left and right, equally puzzled. I stepped forward, yelling to be heard over the din, "I called. I didn't say fire; I said 'there's a terrible liar' and he's right over there. He kidnapped my husband and this young man's father and is holding them against their will."

I couldn't know, of course, but I strongly imagine that no first responders have ever heard such an outlandish story of misunderstanding. I also strongly suspect that they've never been trained for what to do in such a case other than to call off the sirens and send their people back to the stationhouses. Which they did.

A tall, round-faced, double neck–wattled policeman with bars on his shoulders and billed cap advanced to within a few inches of my face. "I'm Chief Darrow. May I ask who you are and what the hell this is all about?"

"Parker here abducted two men. And," I said, crossing fingers behind me, "he threatened me with a weapon." I was going all in based on Stay's findings.

"This woman is nuts! I didn't threaten anybody," Parker said. He looked to a couple of sleepy-eyed fellow smokers for their confirmation, but they merely returned his gaze with a drug-induced glaze before re-sucking their pipes or hookahs or whatever they're called.

"Parker, this woman has made a complaint against you," Chief Darrow said. "Sorry, I know your folks and all, but regulations call for me to frisk you and then we can go down to the station and work this all out."

"You've got no right to touch me," Parker said. "I'm calling my lawyer."

"Parker, you're not being charged with anything. Let me check you out real fast, and we can wrap this up."

Chief Darrow had no more than put a hand on Parker's side when he stopped abruptly. "What's this?" he said, pulling out a small gun from Parker's pocket. "You have a license?"

"Of course I have a license. Not on me, but the law doesn't require me to."

"Parker, a threatening complaint plus a gun in your coat pocket makes this a breach of the peace in my book. I have to place you under arrest, son. Turn around and put your hands together."

"But," I said, "Chief, I don't care about any of this. My husband and Frankie's father are missing. I have evidence that this man knows where they are."

"And what evidence is that, ma'am?"

"Uh, my dog, Stay. Stay is a highly trained tracking device on four feet, er paws."

"Ma'am, let's take one thing at a time. If you come down to the station, we can jot down all your troubles. Don't know if you've heard, but we're mighty short-handed, what with all the holdups."

Stay had been dancing around the entire time and finally bolted for the back entrance to Harry's. I left the Chief calling after me, and

Frankie and I followed our lead detective into the evening humidity.

Stay resumed her nose-sweeping protocol and led us down an alley to the next street over. A peeling white-painted and closed service station right out of the fifties with a "For Sale" sign in the driveway was the object of Stay's fascination. The "For Sale" sign listed the Stone Agency as the outfit to contact. So far, so good.

I tried the door to the station, but it was locked, a small "Closed – Please call again" sign dangling in the window. The three of us made a hasty circle around the building but found no other unsecured entrances. A red brick by the single garage bay caught Frankie's eye.

"We can smash the glass and reach in and turn the knob," he said. So far, I hadn't run afoul of any laws, meaning there was no way I could be indicted for impairing the morals of a teenager, but breaking and entering would surely end my innocence. But so would a dead spouse and father.

"Let me do it," I said. And did. After carefully snaking my hand through some lethal-looking shards of glass, twisting the knob was easy. Entering, I hollered, "Dickie! Eagle!" To no avail.

Stay hadn't bothered to wait for a response. Instead, she dashed to the door with "Restroom" on it, jumped up and down, barking for all she was worth. She knew who was inside, and a second later, so did I.

"Dickie! Eagle!" I cried. Stay began licking Dickie's face, sparing no slobber on my prone husband, hands and feet bound with rope matching that of Eagle's. A gash on Dickie's forehead trailing rivulets of dried blood made me gasp. Frankie began working on the rope with a serious pocketknife while I removed the red handkerchief gags from our loved ones. Stay took the opportunity to reward herself with a pastry from Dickie's coat pocket. "Hey! I was saving that," were the first words from my delinquent spouse.

***

"Hey! I was saving that!" I said, aware that my smile was touching both ears. I'm normally an optimistic sort of guy, but I have to admit I was beginning to harbor a few doubts the last hour or two. In a million years, though, I'd never have expected to be rescued by Mary Ellen, Frankie, and Stay.

"Your husband is out of his league. Should go back to his church. Going to get us all hurt. Stupidest white man I ever met." Eagle was hugging Frankie but addressing Mary Ellen.

The sound of a door crashing open and crunching glass interrupted our little celebration.

"Who're you people?" a young man with "Zenith Security" inscribed on one pocket of his jacket and "Steve" on the other said, pushing Stay away from his crotch.

Mary Ellen pulled Stay away from Steve's business. We haven't found a way to encourage Stay to cease this foul habit, though it is sometimes amusing. "We broke in to rescue these two men who were locked in here by Parker Stone, the real estate man."

Steve shifted from one foot to the other, coughed, and scratched his head – we'd definitely challenged his paygrade. He called someone on his phone who must have said they'd call the police because in no time sirens again blared.

"Had a feeling it would be you again," the man exuding an over-the-top authority said to

Mary Ellen. "Are these the two men you were talking about?"

***

Storrs being a small town, in no more than ten minutes we were seated in a conference room at the police station, Chief Darrow presiding. Stay had been given a doggie biscuit from a cupboard labeled "Canine Control," and was doing her best to ignore the cheap, rock-hard fare.

"Parker took Eagle and me straight to the gas station," I said. "He held a gun on me and made me tie up Eagle. Then I tried to jump him, and he belted me one with the gun. When I came to, I found myself bound and gagged also."

"Parker is bad man," Eagle said. "After knocking out Richard, he bragged about his alibi in case he needed it. Said if anyone linked him to our disappearance, he'd only have to say he was driving us to see a great house that had just come on the market. Said he'd be back for us after dark to take us to a place where we'd never be heard from again. Laughed the whole time he talked. I want to be alone with that man for just a few seconds."

"I still can't believe all this," Chief Darrow said, shaking his head. "Parker's family are good people; he was always a brat, but never in real trouble. Ran the agency well, as far I know. But clearly, there's something bad going on. In fact, if he went to this much trouble to cover up his online real estate scheme, he and Travis and Anne, or the Vern and Kathy you mentioned, must be up to no good in other ways. Anyway, let me get someone in here to write up your statements and you'll be good to go. You want to see a doctor?" he asked me.

"I'm fine," I said. "Wish I'd gotten a picture taken before Mary Ellen cleaned me up. Would've been good for publicity."

Little did I know at that moment, publicity would be the least of my problems.

***

I awoke to Stay's barking and the phone ringing in tandem, but hardly in any kind of recognizable rhythm. A glance through the drapes revealed three of the vans with the satellite dishes that I'd come recently to recognize as common in the neighborhood. I wondered if this was how Paris Hilton began. Or the Kardashians. Famous simply for being famous. I'd done very little to merit all this media focus other than clunk my way through a case and, with Eagle, be given Dynamic Duo status. Still, lots of attention is better than too little.

I let Mary Ellen continue to sleep – earplugs in place defending against my snoring – combed at my hair with my fingers, pulled on a pair of L.L. Bean blue jeans and red-and-black checked flannel shirt, and practiced my best *Cool Hand Luke* smile in the mirror. As on the other occasion of celebrity, I was confident Eagle was being awakened similarly. I opened the front door and was met immediately by a woman with her finger hovering over the doorbell.

"Good morning, Mr. Burgess," she said, "I'm with CNN. Wondering if Mrs. Burgess, Mary Ellen, is available."

"My wife?" I sputtered. "You want to talk to Mary Ellen?"

"Yes, sir. She's CNN's Hero of the Day. Can we have a word with her?"

***

We didn't see the last of CNN for a couple of hours, including a spell when we were on live TV. Our front yard is fairly small but still, there was nary a blade of grass visible as reporters from various media gathered, taking turns with their questions, all interested in how mild-mannered people had become the criminal element's worst nightmare. Stay was a huge hit, coaxing a variety of tidbits from her admirers.

Around 3 o'clock, Eagle called and we compared experiences, his mirroring ours minus the Hero of the Day part. He had a 4 o'clock class to teach, but we agreed to meet for dinner at the Olive Garden in Middletown. In my opinion, at least a couple of people recognized us there: our server – a nice young man who was a student at Wesleyan – and an elderly woman more carrying her walker than leaning on it who entered as we were leaving. But, of course, as I said before, when you're with Eagle, everyone looks at you, at least twice. Little did I know that at that moment I was living the last of my days of relative obscurity. That is, the next morning we were featured in the *Boston Globe*, the *New York Times*, the *Hartford Courant*, the *New Haven Register*, and hundreds of papers that subscribe to the Associated Press. But *USA Today* had the most succinct headline that would shape our lives for years to come: "Meet USA's Dynamic Duo, Wonder Dog, and Church Lady."

The End

About the Author

Will Martin is the pen name of a retired minister living in New England. Married with two children and two grandchildren, he could easily be mistaken for Rev. Richard Burgess.

After Church Mysteries is his first book. Another novel of short stories, *Basically Good People*, will be published later this year.

Acknowledgments

My life as a fiction writer began without a moment's warning. I awoke one summer's day in 2014 with a character and a story in mind and wondered, *what if?* For the next two weeks I clandestinely scribbled a beginning, middle and end. I'd actually written a story. I showed my opus to Jeanne like a school child handing their first crayon creation to a parent. I'd like to report she said, "You're a genius," but I can't. Actually, I don't remember what she said, so wrapped up in my newfound passion was I. But I'm pretty sure she smiled and said something to the effect, "That's not bad. Write another." I was encouraged. Two years and more than three dozen stories later – Jeanne having lovingly critiqued each one – you're reading my "book." I still put "book" in quotation marks because saying I wrote a "book" of fiction sounds presumptuous. But, I guess I have.

Jeanne is, of course, not only my first reader, but first love and forever companion.

There is no more beautiful sound to me than to hear her say, "Well done."

Family members Grant, Diane, Michelle and Maury also patiently read my earliest attempts and lovingly spun their thoughts. God bless them!

Teenage granddaughters Lauren and Katie share the family's passion for reading. I hope they enjoy this Grandpa's attempt to entertain.

Rob Bignell was the first professional to edit my writing. From him I learned the basics of the craft. He, too, majors in encouragement. Thanks, Rob.

Maia Sepp is my Virtual Assistant, which means she's in charge of finding the pros we need for all the parts and crafting the finished product. A lover of words, she is crucial to my self-confidence. If Maia likes it, I know I'm good to go! Thanks, Maia.

Dee Hopkins proofread my manuscript with the keenest of eyes. She also intuited my thin skin in her kind critique. She, too, is a keeper. Thanks, Dee.

Christa Holland designed the cover expertly, and patiently worked with this rookie. She's as much a joy to work with as she is terrific at what she does. Thanks, Christa.

Will Martin
July 2016

Made in the USA
Charleston, SC
31 August 2016